SCARS:
JOHN DEMPSEY

BY BRIAN ANDREWS AND JEFFREY WILSON

Tier One Series

Tier One
War Shadows
Crusader One
American Operator
Red Specter
Collateral

Tier One Origins Novellas

Scars: John Dempsey

OTHER TITLES BY BRIAN ANDREWS

The Calypso Directive
The Infiltration Game
Reset

OTHER TITLES BY JEFFREY WILSON

The Traiteur's Ring
The Donors
Fade to Black
War Torn

SCARS: JOHN DEMPSEY

A TIER ONE ORIGINS NOVELLA

ANDREWS & WILSON

This is a work of fiction. Names, characters, organizations, places, events, and incidents are either products of the author's imagination or are used fictitiously. Any resemblance to actual persons, living or dead, or actual events is purely coincidental.

Copyright © 2020 by Brian Andrews and Jeffrey Wilson

All rights reserved.

No part of this book may be reproduced, or stored in a retrieval system, or transmitted in any form or by any means, electronic, mechanical, photocopying, recording, or otherwise, without express written permission of the publisher.

Trade paperback ISBN: 9798640563689

E-book ASIN: B086LLTKZQ

Cover design by Andrews & Wilson

www.andrews-wilson.com

NOTE TO THE READER

Thank you for downloading *Scars*, the first installment in a new series of novellas called Tier One Origins. Each short features a different Tier One character during a pivotal event in their past before joining Task Force Ember.

Nowhere in this story will you find the name John Dempsey, and for longtime fans of the series that will come as no surprise. But if you haven't read any of the Tier One novels and this novella is your introduction to the series, then *spoiler alert* . . . Jack Kemper *is* John Dempsey.

This story is set in 2006, a decade before the tragic events of Operation Crusader described in *Tier One*, and a decade before the character we all know and love as John Dempsey was born. But Dempsey's hero's heart is easy to recognize, and we hope you enjoy spending a little time with his younger, raw self.

As a thank-you for your purchase of this novella, we're including the first chapter of *Collateral*—book six in the Tier One saga, which goes on sale September 1, 2020, in paperback, e-book, and audiobook.

CHAPTER 1

Al Asad Airbase
Anbar Province, Iraq
June 3, 2006
0450 Local Time

Out of blackness, a thin strip of pink began to materialize to the east as night gave birth to a new day in the Iraqi desert. But that's not what the Team guys sprawled out in the back of the Air Force C-17 transport called this place. For Special Operator First Class Jack Kemper and the rest of his Tier One Navy SEAL brethren, Iraq was the "sandbox," or most days, simply "the suck."

Kemper watched dawn's arrival through one of the few porthole windows toward the front of the jet as the plane banked left, then right—flying an unpredictable pattern of jinks and turns on the approach. War zone landings were nothing like the smooth approach of a civilian airliner, or even the scheduled refueling stop they'd made in Germany. If you couldn't stomach the infil, you had no business being on the plane, let alone in country. The suck, above all else, did not suffer cowards or fools.

Kemper marveled at how much this engagement felt like his first deployment as a SEAL at Team Eight had—feelings of anticipation and excitement competing with self-imposed stress to perform at the highest possible level. After a year in the elite Tier One, every white-side SEAL's dream billet, Kemper was certainly no nugget. He'd graduated from Green Team—the vetting program for the clandestine special missions unit—over a year ago and had since participated in two intense underway exercises and one combat deployment. But this was his first deployment as a squad leader. He felt the weight of being responsible for the other members of his team as they prosecuted the most dangerous terrorists and highest value targets in the War on Terror. Together with their Army, Air Force, and "Other Government Agency" brothers, they were America's most lethal weapons of war.

Gravity returned and pressed him into the orange mesh bench seat as the C-17 leveled from its spiraling descent, rolling wings level just before flaring over the long, wide runway.

Kemper pulled his eyes from the window—the sprawling airbase was mostly in blackout conditions anyway, so there was little to see—and spun his ball cap around forward again on his head. He leaned back against the padded insulation on the wall of the fuselage as the C-17's tires barked their arrival.

"Welcome back to the suck," one of his brothers shouted from the rear of the plane.

On that cue, the smiling face of Kate, his beautiful wife, and their chubby little four-year old boy, Jake, popped into Kemper's mind's eye—a snapshot confirmation of who and what he was doing this for. Or maybe . . . a reminder of the stakes if he failed. After the loss of two teammates from Second Squadron last winter, Kate had broken down and begged him to leave the Teams. Her sobs, and his son's confusion and wide-eyed tears at the family crisis, had burned a hole in his heart. He'd promised he would try—promised to say goodbye to Team life and find another billet. But then, shit spun up again in Iraq, and First Squadron was tapped to go. When he told her the news, Kate didn't cry, just bid him goodbye with a pained, knowing smile.

He'd broken his promise. Now, he couldn't help but wonder if when he came home this time, his wife and son wouldn't be there to greet him.

He quickly chased the morbid thought away. He would make it up to them. When the War on Terror was done—

which it certainly would be soon—the operational tempo would return to manageable. If it didn't, he would find something else in the community that allowed him to be present at home—to be the husband and father they deserved him to be. But right now, he needed to be present here. The intensity of what awaited him on this deployment meant that his teammates in First Platoon, First Squadron needed him to be focused. For the next six months, *they* would be his family.

"'Sup, boss man?" a familiar voice greeted him.

Kemper looked up to see Senior Chief Perry grinning down at him.

"I'm good to go, Senior," Kemper said and meant it. Since flying to Tampa and checking in for this deployment, he'd felt supercharged. He was born for this job and not afraid to say it.

The big man laughed. "Don't get all formal on me now, bro," the platoon NCO said with a smile. "We don't do a lot of that shit here, Jack, as you know, and that ain't changing just 'cause you're leading a team."

Kemper nodded and Perry slapped him hard on the back. Then the salty Senior Chief hiked up his board shorts and padded away, flip-flops smacking as he crossed the steel deck.

"Bro, I can't believe we're finally here," a SEAL they called Romeo said, dropping into the open seat across the aisle from Kemper.

He noticed the man's left foot jumping up and down with nervous energy. Romeo was the nugget at the unit—the youngest SEAL in the squadron, and a new Green Team grad. Romeo was a goofball, but on mission—at least during the exercises and the last underway—he'd proven himself a solid, disciplined shooter. Despite his relative inexperience, he was a tactical savant, seemingly always in the right place at the right time. At a unit where making Chief meant you still took the trash out, earning that kinda reputation was a helluva thing for a nugget. Kemper felt lucky to have him in First Squadron, but training and combat were two different things. Romeo had multiple combat deployments with SEAL Team Seven, but this was the Tier One—he'd need to watch Romeo closely for the first few weeks. He'd never fought beside Romeo, and the nugget was going to be a member of his four-man fire team.

Nothing vets like combat, he thought and patted Romeo on the shoulder.

"You're gonna love these missions," he said. "High tempo, hunting HVTs, every mission matters—it's a frogman's wet dream."

"Fuckin' A," Romeo said, grinning behind his sorry excuse for a beard.

Feeling the C-17 begin to slow as it came out of a turn off the runway, Kemper climbed out of his seat for a stretch. He twisted his shoulders, right and then left to crack his spine, then rolled his wrists and neck, earning him a few additional satisfying pops. Heavy boot steps behind him made Kemper turn, bringing him chest to chest with a grinning Aaron Thiel, his closest friend and teammate at the unit. Kemper smiled large and pulled Thiel in for a hug.

"Dude, I haven't seen you since we left Tampa—you slept through beers in Germany," Kemper said.

Thiel shrugged. "I had to get my beauty rest."

"I hate to break it to you, bro, but no matter how much beauty rest you get, you ain't never gonna be pretty."

Thiel chuckled at the dig. "Actually, I tried Ambien and that shit kicked my ass. Who knew? Gonna do only five milligrams on the way back. Apparently, I tried to snuggle Perry back at our campsite," he said, referring to the hammocks and sleeping bags where most of the SEALs camped out during the flight. "I didn't even wake up when he elbowed me in the face, but I know they ain't lying, because I feel the bruise on my cheek."

Kemper laughed at the picture of his buddy, and fellow squad leader, spooning up to the Senior Chief and getting clocked for it. He and Thiel had graduated BUD/S together—after Thiel fractured his clavicle and had to cycle back to second phase—and had been together since. They'd done SQT together at Team Eight, been roommates in a townhouse on Chick's Beach near Little Creek, and now had screened together for the Tier One.

"Nice," Kemper said. "I think that's Senior's way of sayin' he just wants to be friends."

"Apparently." Thiel laughed, rubbing his cheek.

"Gonna be a good deployment, bro," Kemper said. "Gonna get some. The N2 brief before we left made it sound like there're some serious players who need to spend quality time with the spooks. Gonna be fun making those meetings happen."

"Or just erasing them altogether, bro," Romeo said, joining the two and sliding his black rectangular pack—nearly the size of a twin bed—out from under the mid-aisle bench.

Thiel stared a moment, as if he had something to say, then glanced at the younger SEAL and seemed to change his mind. Instead, he shouldered his own bag and grabbed his weapons case. Kemper did the same and followed him to the back of the plane. He wondered if Thiel was going ask about Kate, but had thought better of it in front of Romeo. Thiel's wife seemed like the perfect Team guy bride—fiercely independent, fun loving, and career oriented. But what did Kemper know? Appearances could be deceiving, and he'd learned to never judge a marriage he wasn't party to. There was a reason the divorce rate in the Teams hovered above fifty percent. It might even be higher in the Tier One—although maybe a unit filled with more senior guys, and marriages that had to survive so much, meant they'd already selected for partners who could weather the storms.

He hoped that was true with Kate.

Kemper followed Thiel down the ramp and out the back of the gargantuan transport jet. A circle of white pickup trucks—like a caravan of covered wagons in the Old West—sat at the base of the ramp. Kemper walked to one of the closer ones, threw his gear in the back, then climbed into the bed. He sat on his rectangular deployment bag like it was a bench seat, and Thiel did the same on the opposite side.

"Hey, bro," a sniper from Second Platoon greeted them, stepping out of the driver's seat and scratching at his full beard.

"'Sup, Ted?" Kemper said. "Ya'll been getting some?"

"Yep," the sniper said with a grin. "Operations almost every night. Also doing some cool overwatch stuff. Gonna take you to drop your shit, then I'll grab the guys who just got back and we'll all head to breakfast. Don't wanna get stuck in the long line for the omelet bar."

"War is hell," Thiel agreed.

"Amen," the sniper said as four more guys, including Romeo and Perry, crammed into the bed of the truck.

"Join you?" a voice called behind them.

Kemper looked over his shoulder to see Lieutenant Commander Neal Mercer jogging over from the plane.

"Sure, man," the sniper said with the informality Kemper loved about the team. Downrange, they were just a collection of warriors. "Up front, we're full in back."

"We got yer gear, Neal," Perry said and grabbed the officer's bag while Thiel hoisted his weapons case, both added to the pile of luggage in the bed.

Moments later they were screaming down the taxiway, the dry air cool on Kemper's skin, but the growing light on the horizon reminding him that they were only a few hours away from temperatures over one hundred and twenty degrees in the shade.

"But hey, it's a dry heat," Thiel said, slapping Kemper's knee. He'd read his mind. "And anyway, we'll sleep through that shit. I'm planning to PT before breakfast every night when we get back and be in the rack before it tops one hundred."

Kemper laughed. SEALs were vampires, after all.

When they reached the Tier One compound, Ted hopped out of the driver's seat, spun the combination to a simple padlock securing the twelve-foot-high fence, then dragged the gate open wide enough for the caravan of pickups to drive through. Inside the perimeter a cluster of long, low structures was laid out around a large square building topped with myriad antennas and satellite dishes. In back, two rows of gleaming white shower/toilet trailers served the bunkhouses. Kemper knew that the real security was not the silly padlock—he still remembered the combination from his last deployment—it was the understated nature and anonymity of the facility itself. Only cleared personnel from the main base were allowed up to the flight line, and fewer still to the southwest corner of the field—both of which were guarded by checkpoints. Few personnel on the base had any idea who they were, or that the most elite Joint Special Operations Command counterterrorist operators in the world ate breakfast beside them in the chow halls. The compound bore no signage and didn't appear on any map or org chart. The operators themselves dressed in civilian clothes whenever they left their compound—5.11 cargo pants and plaid shirts or T-shirts, mostly—and sported long hair and beards. To the uninitiated, they looked like any other contractors doing maintenance, providing communications support, working in the base fire department, or driving trucks.

The secret nature of their work was all the security they needed.

Kemper's stomach growled.

A big breakfast, a workout, and then some sleep after checking their gear sounded perfect. But as tempting as the thought of passing out in his rack with a full belly was, he knew he should call Kate before she put Jake to bed for the night. Once he'd made that call, he'd be able to immerse himself guilt free in the business of being a covert operator.

And if he was really lucky . . . when the sun went down again, First Squad would get to kit up and go to work.

CHAPTER 2

Al Asad Airbase
Anbar Province, Iraq
June 4
1915 Local Time

Kemper shuffled after Thiel and Perry into the large square wooden building that for some reason reminded him of an old-fashioned schoolhouse. Maybe it was the wood walls, wood ceiling, and wood floors with matching wooden benches that completed the image for him.

"Hey," Thiel said over his shoulder as they pushed through the door, "I meant to ask you at dinner—what have you heard from Munn? Is that asshole really in medical school?"

Kemper laughed. "Yeah. I talked to him on the phone just before we left, and he's jealous as shit."

Munn had been the 18-Delta SEAL medic with them at Team Eight and had lived in the townhouse on the beach with them for a year and a half, before being the first to fall off into marriage. He'd also served at the Tier One for two years, leaving just as Kemper was making it through Green Team so he could chase his dream of becoming a trauma surgeon.

"Really?" Thiel said.

"Oh yeah. I think he thought that things over here were gonna wind down, and he didn't wanna be an old man by the time he became a doc. But now that the shit's hitting the fan, he sounded like he regrets the decision."

Thiel laughed as they took seats on one of the long wooden benches. "Probably gonna get fat," he said.

"Better not," Kemper said as SEALs and support personnel crowded in around them. "He's still in the Navy and says he's coming back to the Teams when he's done."

"Yeah, right. He'll get a taste of that sweet life as a rich doctor and we'll never see him again. Big gate around his mansion—paying people to read his mail and shit."

Kemper laughed, but he knew better. As tight as he and Aaron Thiel were, Dan Munn was probably the best friend he'd ever have. Munn was a genius and a warrior. He'd gone to medical school so he could treat his fellow SEALs at the highest level, but the trident tattooed on the man's chest went way deeper—all the way to his soul. He'd be back. And he would always be a Team guy in Kemper's mind.

"Okay, gentlemen," Lieutenant Commander Mercer said as he took the podium. It was made from the same wood as the walls and floor, rendering it almost invisible until someone stepped behind it. "Instead of doing our normal nineteen hundred intel brief, I'm kicking things off a little early today. We have some new and actionable intelligence on a serious fuck stick who made our tasking docket for tonight."

The task unit commander picked up a remote, and the large monitor on the wall behind him—starkly high tech in the wooden hut—came to life. "This is Mahmood Bin Jabbar," he said.

Kemper stared at the dark-eyed terrorist—he and the other SEALs in the room burning the image into their brains—and wondered about the source of the photo. The image was a headshot, the terrorist Mujahideen leader staring straight at the camera.

"Bin Jabbar is going to be in Ramadi tonight—arrived this morning, in fact—and we have capture/kill orders on this joker and the contingent of sadistic assholes who travel with him. The emphasis here is on capture, but every SEAL comes home safe tonight, so do what ya gotta do."

"Neal, I thought from the N3 brief that this cat was running the show—and the flow of weapons—from way out west near the Syrian border. What's he doing in Ramadi?" Perry asked.

"Good memory, Senior," Mercer said with a nod to his LCPO. "And one of the reasons why we really want this dude alive if we can get him. His arrival is unexpected. Many of the fractures between regional tribes seem on the mend, probably because of the escalated violence in Ramadi and the resurgence of sectarian killings there and in Fallujah. The enemy of my enemy and all that shit."

"Isn't Abu Musab al-Zarqawi basically running the show in Ramadi?" Thiel asked.

Mercer nodded. "That's right, and we're seeing Zarqawi pulling together rival tribes and leaders, coalescing them under the flag of beating back the Western invaders. We don't know this for certain, but the thinking is that Bin Jabbar is here for this reason. SEAL Team Three has been operating in Ramadi for months, along with the 3/8 Marines, and both are reporting rapidly escalating violence in recent weeks. Zarqawi's shitheads control the government center, the hospital, and large swaths of the city. Our leadership is bringing in First and Second Brigade Combat Teams from Tal Afar, as well as First Armor, to launch a massive offensive in Ramadi to take control back. Obviously, we have Team Three beating the bushes looking for Zarqawi, and if they locate him, expect capture/kill tasking for that asshole as well. But for now, we need to find out what level of support and cooperation is going on in Ramadi between Zarqawi and the other faction leaders. When we see a guy like Bin Jabbar come to town from way out near Al Qa'im, then we know something's up."

"Do we think we may get a line on Zarqawi on this op?" Perry asked, his voice eager and ready.

"Who knows? We'll get a brief on the latest intel in a minute from Second Squadron's N3 in theater, Lieutenant Felsk." A thin and very attractive woman with the build of a triathlete raised her hand from the front row, a loose introduction for the recent arrivals. "A twofer would be awesome, obviously, but right now the assets on the ground believe tonight's meeting is between Bin Jabbar and one of Zarqawi's lieutenants. We don't have a handle on Zarqawi's midlevel personnel, so anyone you can snatch off the X could be of tremendous value."

Kemper felt his heart rate pick up. This, right here, was why he'd worked the last few years toward the singular goal of making the Tier One. This was a mission that, if properly executed, could change the course of the battle for Ramadi. With conventional forces preparing for a major assault and operators from Team Three prosecuting targets, conducting intelligence, surveillance, and reconnaissance, and rounding up known players, a successful operation like this could be a game changer. Capturing Bin Jabbar could save countless American and civilian Iraqi lives in the weeks to come—including their brothers from Team Three and the Marine Corps who were deep in the suck.

"This op is going to First Platoon with Perry at the helm," Mercer announced.

"Yes!" Thiel said and shot Kemper a thumbs-up. For their first mission as squad leaders, they'd landed one helluva big fish.

"I'll be in the passenger seat on second stick inbound," Mercer continued. "I'll coordinate with Team Three leadership since Three will be our backup on this op. We're hitching a flight with our cousins from the 160th out to COP Falcon, but this is an urban assault into the center of the city. We'll have the 3/8 Marines, Kilo Company, patrolling the block ahead of us, with Lima Company backing them up and Team Three snipers in overwatch. The plan is for First Platoon to infil with the guys from the Stryker Brigade already operating in the city, since they'll know the roads and geography tight."

The more he heard, the more excited Kemper was getting—and it wasn't lost on him how high the stakes were for his first operation as a Tier One squad leader.

"I'm gonna turn things over to Lieutenant Felsk now for the latest intelligence updates. Once the AFSOC and Night

Stalker guys join, we'll do a full mission brief. But first, I got someone who wanted to say a few words." Mercer nodded to the back of the room and said, "Fellas, make some room for Captain Jarvis, our CSO."

Boots pounded the wooden floor and Kemper looked over his shoulder as the legendary Navy SEAL and head of the Tier One command strode to the front. All around the room, men began to rise, springing to attention as this particular group of warriors almost never did.

"Sit down, sit down," Jarvis barked as he shook hands with Mercer and took the podium. "Don't be a bunch of assholes."

A swell of laughter rumbled across the room, and the assembled SEALs took their seats again.

Jarvis was dressed in desert cammies—his pant legs untucked over Keen hiking boots—and wore a Sig Sauer P226 in a drop holster on his right thigh. SEALs from any generation revered the man at the podium, the most decorated SEAL in history, who had spent more than half his career in the JSOC community and had been hunting jihadi terrorists with the Israelis before "jihadi terrorist" was even part of the American lexicon.

"So, this is the first op for you guys from First Platoon, relieving your brothers who are headed home—albeit by way of Afghanistan," he said, earning him another wave of laughter. "I wanted to take a minute to impress on you the importance of this operation—which of course is why it comes to us, the best damn operators on earth. This asshole"—he gestured with a thumb at Bin Jabbar—"may look like some loser jacking off in his mother's basement, but don't be fooled. He is well deserving of the 'high-value target' designation we've given him. He's been in this fight longer than any of you, working with anyone who shares his lust for killing infidels, especially the American devils in his country. Unlike many Mujahideen, this dude gets his hands bloody. We have tapes of him personally executing hundreds of people, and one particularly disturbing video of him beheading two women with a butcher knife while their husbands watched—then shooting the husbands in the face. He is a special breed of sociopath and surrounds himself with others just like him. If Zarqawi is embracing this type of jihadist, then it's an ominous sign for how low things will get in Ramadi in the coming months."

Jarvis paced away from the podium.

"Everything I've told you—along with what will be shared by Lieutenant Felsk in a moment—will make you want to kill this motherfucker. And that's good, because death is what Bin Jabbar deserves . . . but don't," he said, turning back to face them. "Don't kill this guy if you can take him alive. Not only will the intelligence in Bin Jabbar's head save countless American and partner nation lives, but the deep dark hole we'll send him down is the just punishment he deserves. A headshot gets this guy off too easy. Do you understand?"

Jarvis paused, his hands clasped behind his back, and looked out at the room of bearded SEALs and support teams.

"Hooyah?" he challenged.

"Hooyah," the Tier One SEALs answered in unison.

"Go get some," Jarvis said, shook Mercer's hand, and then pounded his hiking boots across the wooden floor toward the rear exit. As Jarvis passed, he nodded at Kemper, a fire in his eyes. "Mr. Kemper . . ."

"Sir." Kemper nodded back.

"What the hell was that?" Thiel asked after Jarvis had left the room. "You guys got some secret history I should know about?"

"No idea," Kemper said, shaking his head in disbelief that the CSO would remember his name. He'd only interacted with the man once, and that was at his screening board. "But the pressure sure as hell is on now."

Thiel nodded and they both returned their attention to the podium, where Lieutenant Felsk was starting her detailed intelligence brief.

CHAPTER 3

COP Falcon
Ramadi, Iraq
June 5
0045 Local Time

In the dark, it was hard to say how much Ramadi had changed since Kemper had passed through in 2004. On that deployment with Eight, he and his teammates had helped rout high-value terrorist targets who were escaping the American offensive in Fallujah and communities clustered around Al Wadi Thar Thar to the north. Back then, there had been plenty of shitheads to go around, but Ramadi hadn't been the stronghold of jihadists it was today. The Jordanian-born Abu Musab al-Zarqawi had been busy, refashioning Ramadi into a mecca for terrorists. After declaring his allegiance to bin Laden and running a terrorist training camp in Afghanistan, the charismatic Zarqawi had convinced his legion of violent followers that Ramadi was where they would take their stand against the devils from the West. Since his arrival, much of the civilian population had fled the city. Now that the Americans were setting up to reclaim it—with memories of the complete and utter destruction that had occurred in Fallujah still fresh in the Iraqi zeitgeist—most of those who remained had followed suit.

But leadership meant for this time to be different, or so they'd said, with neighborhood-by-neighborhood routing of the insurgents and priority given to protecting civilians and infrastructure. The Western alliance had learned in 2004 that it was of little value to forge relationships with local partners through a promise of liberation, only to hand over a steaming pile of rubble to the once and future occupants.

"I'm hearing Team Three is up to their necks in shit already," Thiel said from beside him as the Blackhawk operated by the Army's elite 160th Special Operations Air Regiment—the famous Night Stalkers—flared over the landing pad just outside the wall of COP Falcon, the small Naval Special Warfare combat outpost. "So, I'm sure they'll be thrilled to see us coming."

"I don't know," Kemper said, shifting his rifle on his chest and preparing to step out of the helo. "I never minded helping the Tier One guys when I was at Eight."

"Yeah, well," Thiel said, bending low in respect of the still-spinning rotor above their heads, "we weren't wading up to our necks in the suck like they are. They know what's going on in Ramadi better than we do, I'd argue."

"True," Kemper said, following his friend to where a group of men stood in a loose circle by a gate.

Moments later the two helicopters were swallowed by the night, and the eight SEALs and their senior officer, Lieutenant Commander Mercer, were greeted by four SEALs from Team Three.

"Rusty Perry," the Senior Chief introduced himself, shaking hands with a tall, thin operator in dirty cargo pants and a maroon Virginia Tech sweatshirt. Sometimes the nights in the desert were cool enough to warrant long sleeves, despite the ungodly daytime heat.

"Jim Norris," the lead Team Three NCO said. "Glad to have you fellas here. We're a little thin right now—got some guys running a thing out west of the city—but we can augment your stick with a couple of shooters if you need. We already committed to your Head Shed to have two Team snipers up in the area, and maybe you can give them an update before they roll out."

"Appreciate the offer," Perry said. "We got the shooters we need, but thanks for the snipers setting up ahead of our op." He turned to Kemper. "Jack, can you give a quick brief and recap for Jim's guys so they can set up?"

"Will do, boss," Kemper said.

"'Sup, Romeo?" a younger SEAL beside the NCO said, leaning in and smiling. "Thought that was you. Surprised to see you here, since the good money had you washing out of Green Team."

Romeo laughed and leaned in for a hug. "Hey, bro! How are you, man? You guys getting some down here?"

"Fixing to," the SEAL replied. "Sounds like some serious shit coming down in the next couple of days."

"Hell, yeah," Romeo said, and the two warriors high-fived each other.

"I think I know you," the other guy beside Norris said, staring at Kemper in the low light. "Team Eight, right? We crossed paths at second phase of jump—out at HALO school—remember?"

Kemper looked closely, then smiled. "Yeah, yeah—I remember you. Idaho boy, right? Family has some big ranch or some shit?"

The SEAL laughed. "Montana, but pretty good memory. I'm Alan . . ."

"Jack," Kemper said, shaking Alan's extended hand.

"This way," Norris said, waving them to follow. "We've got Marines from the 3/8 coming over with wheels to get you to the X. They're your close-contact QRF, but also know we have a squad kitted up and ready here, if needed."

"Appreciate that, Jim," Perry said as Kemper followed the SEAL called Alan through the gate.

"Gonna get busy here pretty soon, I think," Alan was saying. "If we can find Zarqawi, maybe we can stop the shit storm before it gets worse, but dude, it's already bad. These fuck sticks following Zarqawi are animals—killing kids and stringing them up on walls if they think the dads are cooperating, murdering whole families in their homes, planting IEDs all over the city. They've killed five times as many Iraqis as they have Americans, probably more. I'm telling you, the shit we've seen is absolutely inhuman. It's like an alternate fucking reality."

"Yeah," was all Kemper replied, having already tightened his grip on his rifle at the mention of kids being killed. That got to him in a visceral way. He'd seen some serious violence and sadism on his prior deployments, but the briefing they'd had on Ramadi suggested this place was a whole new level of suck. "Maybe this op will help us move the needle in the other direction."

"Amen to that," Alan said.

I'm going to get this asshole Bin Jabbar, Kemper silently promised himself. *I'm going to take him tonight . . . and I'm going to take him alive.*

With the intel their spooky OGA brethren would harvest from Bin Jabbar, they'd get a location on Zarqawi and go after him next. And with any luck, it would be Kemper and his guys—not SEAL Team Three—that put the bullet in Zarqawi's head and turned the tide in Ramadi.

CHAPTER 4

Nazal Old City Neighborhood
Ramadi, Iraq
June 5
0232 Local Time

Kemper pressed his shoulder against the wall beside the target building's front door—his SOPMOD M4 held at a forty-five-degree angle, index finger tapping the trigger guard. He watched while the SEAL called Sandman pressed a small breacher charge into the doorframe beside the knob. For this op, Kemper was both squad leader and team leader, with Senior only taking over if things went to hell or he became incapacitated. Hitting the front was the four-man fire team consisting of Kemper, Perry, Romeo, and Sandman. Thiel and three other SEALs would breach simultaneously from the back.

With the charge set, Kemper watched Sandman crab backward along the wall, trailing the det cord in front of him, until Perry tapped him on the shoulder to stop. Kemper looked to Perry to make the call, but the Senior Chief nodded, letting Kemper lead his chalk as promised.

"Choctaw Two—Choctaw One is set," Kemper whispered into the boom mike beside his mouth, alerting Thiel that they were ready to breach.

In the corner of his eye, Kemper saw a boy, perhaps eight years old, walk past on the other side of the narrow street. He turned and met the kid's gaze, finding more curiosity than malice. He nodded at the boy, who waved, then Kemper made a shooing gesture with his left hand. The young Iraqi stopped in his tracks, stared for a moment, then ran off quietly down the street.

"Choctaw Two is set," came Thiel's reply.

Thiel and his three SEALs were positioned in an alley outside a stone wall surrounding the small courtyard at the rear of the building. The target was a typical two-story Ramadi city dwelling, one of a dozen crammed wall-to-wall along the street. Even with the Marines holding all four corners of the block, managing and marking every local on or in every sidewalk, courtyard, rooftop, or window was impossible. Kemper felt like a fish in a barrel.

"God, Choctaw One," he said, quietly querying the two snipers from SEAL Team Three somewhere above them. "Anyone on approach?"

"Ya'll got a few randoms wandering around," said a calm voice with a Texas twang—their overwatch sniper from Team Three—"but nothing armed or organized headed toward your pos. We got yer six, Choctaw."

Kemper took a long, slow breath. His spidey sense was screaming, but there was nothing left to do but breach and hit the target.

"Three . . . two . . . one . . ."

As he said "one," the doorknob moved, someone turning it from the inside. The breacher charge fired with a dull *whump*, followed immediately by the shrill howl of a man in agony. Kemper popped up from his knee and moved in a combat crouch, meeting Sandman at the door. Feeling Romeo's hand on his trailing left shoulder, he nodded to Sandman.

What remained of the front door was already swinging open as Sandman crossed the threshold and cleared left. Kemper followed him in, scanning the room through the holosight on his rifle. He sighted a man hunched at the waist and clutching a bloody stump where his right hand had once been, then Sandman's 5.56 round tore the man's head apart. Kemper swiveled, clearing right. Movement in the corner morphed into a man raising an AK-47, and Kemper squeezed twice as he shifted the dot to the center of the target's grey tunic-covered chest, both rounds hitting center mass and dropping the jihadist to the floor. Kemper continued his right corner sweep as he moved, found no other threats, then turned back to the left and surged forward as Romeo and Perry advanced into the center lane opened by him and Sandman.

A dark stairwell rose directly ahead of him, and Kemper dragged his red dot up the shadow-shrouded stairs. He sighted an armed, older man backpedaling three-quarters of the way up the stairs and dropped him with a headshot.

Gunfire blazed from his left, coming from either Romeo or Perry. Kemper took a knee for a lower angle up the stairs, intent on keeping any upper-level tangos out of the fight until they'd finished securing the downstairs.

"Choctaw Two is coming over the wall—you have movement upstairs, One."

Yeah, no shit, he thought as three figures appeared at the top of the staircase with AK-47s. All three insurgents opened fire, hosing down the center of the room where Perry and Romeo were advancing. Kemper held position and returned fire, wounding one as the three terrorists scrambled to take cover and disappeared.

Then the world suddenly turned very bright, very hot, and very loud—

The explosion knocked Kemper backward, but he caught himself. Perry and Romeo, however, seemed to take the brunt of the blast, Perry hitting the wall beside the door and sliding down to the floor on his ass, and Romeo landing half in and half out of the ruined front doorway. Kemper shook his head clear, sighted back up the stairs, and fired a three-round burst into the smoke and dust billowing down on him, earning a scream from above. A teenaged fighter, barely old enough to carry the AK-47 slung over his shoulder, tumbled down the stairs and landed dead beside him. Kemper fired another burst, but whoever else was up there had wisely pulled back.

He drifted left to look around the stairs, and that's when he saw what had actually been blown up—the entire back wall of the house was gone, nothing but a charred and gaping hole looking out into the courtyard. Agonizing worry hit him like a punch to his gut. Had Thiel and his team been in the courtyard when that thing blew?

"Choctaw Two, SITREP," he choked into his Peltor boom mike, and then honked a big cough to clear his lungs of dust and debris. While he waited on a reply, he glanced over his shoulder at Perry and Romeo and called, "You guys okay?"

"All good," Perry said. "Checking Romeo."

"Sandman has shrapnel in his leg," Sandman called. "But I'm in the fight."

"One—Two," came Thiel's strained voice in his headset. "That explosion hit when we were coming over. Took out half the wall and blew us back into the alley. I have casualties here . . ." A three-round burst of M4 fire filled the air from behind the house, followed by another. "Shit, One, tangos are squirting. Repeat, our HVT is squirting out the back!"

"Romeo smacked his head pretty good," Perry called out. "He's out of the fight."

"Sandman," Kemper hollered, firing another three-round burst as he rose to his feet and surged forward. "Cover the stairs. I'm going to finish clearing this level and sweep the courtyard. See if I can catch these assholes."

"Check," Sandman said.

Visibility improved for Kemper as the smoke billowed out of the house and the dust settled onto the floor. He saw movement through the massive hole at the back of the house as he advanced. He moved fast, in a low tactical crouch, scanning left and right.

"Choctaw One for Apache," he called to the Captain leading the 3/8 Marines securing the block perimeter. "We need immediate CASEVAC at our pos and security to close in and tighten the noose."

His senses on high alert, he reached the giant maw in the back wall. Sighting through the hole into the courtyard, Kemper spied the back of an enemy fighter. The terrorist was sighting over his rifle and advancing toward where Thiel's men were no doubt recovering from being blown off the wall by the explosion. Kemper fired, hitting the shooter between the shoulder blades; the man pitched forward and skidded on his chest through the dirt. Kemper put a second round in the back of the longhaired jihadi's head and stepped through the hole into the courtyard, clearing left, then right. With the ground level clear, he swiveled, scanned up, and found a target. He fired twice at a jihadi trying to escape by climbing down a drainpipe. Kemper's rounds flew true and the man fell headfirst. If the gunshot hadn't killed him, the impact—which split his head open like a melon—certainly did.

"Choctaw One, Apache—sending wheels and medical for CASEVAC now," the Marine Captain reported.

"Copy."

With the courtyard clear, he leaped over a pile of rubble and made for a collapsed section of the perimeter wall.

"Choctaw Variable, One—if you have eyes, call Custer for me," Kemper said, using the code name they had assigned to Bin Jabbar. In that moment, he decided he would not let whatever casualties his team had suffered on this hit be for nothing. He took a knee beside the gap in the perimeter wall and popped his head around the corner for a split-second look, pulling back to register what he'd seen: two SEALs on combat knees beside a third lying on the ground, a fourth administering aid.

"One—that you?" called a voice from the other side.

Kemper rose, rounded the breach, and came face to face with Thiel, the SEAL's face smeared with dirt, soot, and blood.

"Three of them squirted out the second story, cleared the wall, and headed north," Thiel said. "One looked like Bin Jabbar, but I can't be sure."

Kemper nodded and quickly surveyed the downed SEALs.

"Davidson's left leg is shredded all to shit, bro," Thiel said and looked over his shoulder to where Epperson, the SEAL medic, was working on their fallen teammate. "Jacked up his arm, too, but that leg is bad."

Damn it.

He doubted any tangos remained upstairs—blowing out the back wall had clearly been Bin Jabbar's contingency plan in the event of a raid. But no point in anyone getting shot in the back in the event he was wrong.

"Apache, come to the rear where we have an urgent surgical," Kemper relayed. "Three, Four, and Five—hold the stairs and then move to the rear for exfil when Apache calls in."

He looked closer at Thiel and noted blood running in triple rivulets down the side of his friend's face. "You good, bro?"

Thiel wiped blood from his face with the back of his hand, looking at the mess, and squeezed his eyes shut before opening them again. "All good, I think." Then with more confidence, he added, "Still in the fight."

"Coordinate the evacuation, bro," Kemper said to him, and began quickstepping in a low crouch toward the corner of the perimeter wall.

"Where are you going, Jack?" Thiel called.

"Just gonna take a look around the corner to see if I can see them."

"Dude, wait . . ." Thiel called after him. "I'll come with you."

"No, stay here and set up security. Every asshole in the neighborhood will be heading this way any second," he said. "I'll be right back."

Kemper took off in a sprint up the narrow, dark street to the north . . . the only place that Bin Jabbar could have gone.

CHAPTER 5

As Kemper's boots pounded the uneven pavement, two voices screamed in his head simultaneously. The first told him to take a deep breath, reconnect with the team, and stop chasing terrorists alone through the streets of a jihadi-controlled city. But the other voice insisted he needed to kill the assholes who'd just torn up his brothers. When he spotted the three men, the one in a blue tunic flanked by two heavily armed shooters, the second voice won.

Kemper drifted to the left side of the road for cover, leaned into his combat crouch, and picked up the pace.

"Choctaw Variable, One," he called, checking in with his command and control. "I have eyes on Custer and I'm pursuing."

A long pause lingered on the circuit as he closed the gap, and he brought his M4 up to drop the two shooters flanking the primary. But before he could sight in, the trio broke left at the corner, heading straight toward the highway that divided the city into north and south sectors. Once Bin Jabbar crossed that road, he'd be in al-Zarqawi's neighborhood . . .

"Fuck," he hissed and sprinted to the corner. "Variable, Choctaw One—I need eyes right now or I'll lose Custer."

"Choctaw One, you need to—" an irritated Lieutenant Commander Mercer started to say, but then cut off.

A moment later, a new voice was in his headset—familiar, but he couldn't immediately place it.

"Choctaw One, Variable—we're getting you eyes in five seconds. You are not to cross the highway and do not engage if you are uncertain of the numbers. Confirm you understand."

The last words made clear who was speaking. The Tier One CSO, Captain Kelso Jarvis, was now in his headset. Kemper felt a wave of uncertainty. The boss had cleared him to continue, but then he had already broken a half dozen major rules by going this far, so why not, right? He had a feeling he had just fucked up so bad that his first op as a squad leader might well be his last day at the Tier One.

"Copy, sir," he said, breathing hard as he scanned left and right down the dark and empty street. Short stucco houses were crammed together only inches apart along the narrow road. A young man suddenly appeared in front of him, freezing and dropping the paper cup in his hand, eyes wide with surprise.

Kemper pointed his M4 at the boy's chest.

"Arini yudik," Kemper growled, and the boy complied, showing the palms of both hands. But a wave of anger and hatred spread over his face—one Kemper instantly recognized. This boy saw Kemper and the Americans not as liberators, but as invaders. This boy would tell someone about the American soldier in the alley. Kemper scanned the boy's torso for bulges indicative of a suicide vest or weapons. Seeing none, he commanded the boy to run away in Arabic. When the boy just stood there, glaring, Kemper sighted in on the young man's face. *"Yarkud,"* he barked, and now the boy did just that, running down the street, glancing over his shoulder in fear of being shot in the back.

"They went inside, Choctaw One," came a cool voice from the Tactical Operations Center back at COP Falcon. He pictured Captain Jarvis standing behind the radio talker, arms crossed against his chest, supervising everything unfolding. "Left at the corner, two doors down."

"Check," he said just as a bullet whizzed past his head, tearing a chunk of stucco from the corner of the house beside him. Kemper whirled, dropped to a knee, and sighted on a shadowy figure by a beat-up tan Mercedes with only three tires. He squeezed the trigger twice. His rifle barked out two 5.56 rounds, which hit side by side in the man's forehead, and the patrolling jihadi fell to the ground, his AK-47 clattering beside him.

Where there's one, there's more, he thought, and knew he was almost out of time.

"How many inside, Variable?" Kemper gasped, as he spun around and quickstepped toward the target. He rounded the corner, sighting over his rifle. His thighs were on fire from the lactic acid building up from the constant surging in a combat crouch, like he was doing his nine-hundredth squat in the gym. "Just the three who went in, or is it a party?"

"Hold on and I can retask the drone to get you thermals."

Kemper paused fifteen feet short of the target door. He'd assumed Variable was vectoring him behind Bin Jabbar based on the drone feed, but now realized they were using the drone for security on the SEALs waiting for exfil and the 3/8 Marines still holding the perimeter in what was about to become a city-wide gun battle if they didn't get the fuck out of the neighborhood. He'd followed the enemy fighters to the edge of the perimeter. If they snuck another block north, they'd be at the highway and escape to where Zarqawi had an enormous presence. Either Kemper engaged them here or the op was over.

He decided he couldn't wait.

"Let me know if they squirt out the back door," Kemper said as he converged on the door. "And have the 3/8 collapse in on me to pick up me and Custer."

"Roger, Choctaw One," the cool voice came back. If the operator realized the wild optimism Kemper's order relied on, he didn't express it.

At the door now, Kemper paused, his weapon at forty-five degrees as he looked through his NVGs at the partially cracked-open door. If Bin Jabbar and his seconds were hiding in there, Kemper might well get them.

He hesitated.

I'm alone, with no backup, in the middle of terrorist country, about to breach a door into a possible hornet's nest. I'm either going to die or be a hero . . .

And the deciding factor was on the other side of this door.

He exhaled, took a step backward, and kicked the door in.

A tornado of adrenaline, Kemper surged into the room . . . but two feet past the threshold, he froze. Instead of facing three jihadis, he found himself surrounded by seven heavily armed, heavily bearded men. In their surprise at this unexpected turn of events, none of them had their weapons raised.

"Bin Jabbar, 'ant at mey," Kemper barked, ordering Bin Jabbar to come with him. *"Akhbar rajalak bi'iilqa aslihatahum!"*

Another idea came to him—a feint that might give him the seconds he needed.

A man of Bin Jabbar's status would speak English . . .

"I have him, plus six tangos," Kemper said into his boom mike, pretending he had an entire team outside the door. "Secure the four corners. Ten men behind and ten on the street as we come out."

The message he was trying to send was clear: *I've got twenty men, asshole, so just give up.*

Mujahideen like Bin Jabbar rarely practiced what they preached. The fight-to-the-death allegiance they demanded from their followers did not apply to them. He'd seen ruthless terrorists cry like babies at the first question of an interrogation, so, maybe this one would give up instead of dying, right?

For a moment, he thought his ruse might actually have worked. Most of the men, apparently, did not speak English and looked to Bin Jabbar for guidance.

"Let's go, Bin Jabbar," Kemper barked at the man in the blue tunic.

"Say again, Choctaw?" a voice queried in his ear. "The 3/8 Marines are still three or four mikes out. Recommend you hold . . . oh, shit, we see what you're doing."

And then Bin Jabbar laughed—a long, deep laugh from his belly—and the men with him began to laugh as well.

As their weapons came up, Kemper's brain prioritized his targets by their speed, distance, and angle. He spun in a slow clockwise half circle as he fired rapidly from his SOPMOD M4, dropping three bad guys before any of them fired. He shifted back and slid hard left as the first shooter fired, and felt the heat from the 7.62 round that whipped past his cheek as he put one of his own rounds through the man's forehead, splitting the top of his head open like a canoe.

Three left...

As he sighted on the blue tunic, a powerful arm knocked Kemper's rifle off target, and his bullet sailed wide, missing Bin Jabbar's smiling, bearded face. A second terrorist, who'd been closing on him from the other side, grabbed his left arm and jerked it violently, sending searing pain through his shoulder. Working together, Bin Jabbar's two bodyguards tore the rifle from Kemper's grip.

Instinct kicked in—guided by a decade of close-quarters combat and grappling training—and Kemper dropped straight down, kicking his left leg out in front of him and landing hard on his right knee. The move freed his right arm, the terrorist preferring to retain his grip on the rifle, but his left arm remained held fast in the vise-like grip of the man on his left. With eye-blurring speed, Kemper pulled the Sig Sauer

P226 from the drop holster on his right thigh, raised it, and fired blindly left. Meanwhile, the jihadi on his right spun his M4 in a tight circle, twisting the strap—which was unfortunately still around Kemper's neck—into a noose. He heard an animalistic scream as the round from his Sig hit the man to his left, but the wounded terrorist kept a grip on his left arm.

A flash of light made him look up just in time to see a long, curved blade slashing down. Bin Jabbar had gone savage—his face twisted in a demonic, vulpine snarl as he wielded the knife. Kemper threw all of his weight to the right, freeing his left arm and toppling the man beside him. The curved dagger—like something from *The Arabian Nights*—missed his neck. Kemper avoided decapitation, but the arm he'd raised to block the strike did not fare well. The blade bit into his left forearm just below the crease of his elbow. He felt it slice deep, carving him to the bone as he fell. Bin Jabbar deftly worked the blade, spiraling the cut from outside to inside, from the elbow halfway down to his wrist.

Kemper landed with a grunt on top of the man to his right, who'd lost his balance and tumbled during the melee. With the strap now loose around his neck, Kemper had some room to move. He fired another round left and watched the top of that man's head evaporate in a cloud of white bone, dark blood, and chunks of grey. Still clutching the Sig, with all his strength he drove his right elbow backward and felt the cheekbone of the fighter beneath him collapse with an audible crunch.

He scrambled to his knees and fired his Sig at the fleeing Bin Jabbar. His first bullet tore away a chunk of doorframe three inches from Bin Jabbar's head as the asshole disappeared out the back. He unloaded three more rounds into the void and tried to pursue, but the rifle sling stopped him as the man on the ground tried once more to choke him. Kemper pushed up and then dropped his full weight down center mass on the jihadi. He felt the nauseating crunch as the man's rib cage gave way under the blow, like a piano had dropped on his chest. Instead of a scream, all Kemper heard was a wet, gurgling grunt.

Kemper lowered his head, spun out of the rifle sling, and exploded to his feet, pistol up again. He tried to raise his left arm to steady his shooting hand, but the hand just slapped the side of his pistol uselessly.

Then he felt it—the hot spray of blood across his face—and he looked down to see arterial blood arcing up rhythmically from his flayed left forearm.

"Son of a bitch," he muttered and took a knee, pressing his left arm against his side to stem the bleeding.

Instinctively, he turned clockwise, saw the badly wounded terrorist he had dropped his weight on crawling toward his own rifle, and shot him twice in the back of the head.

Getting woozy now, Kemper stood, stumbled, took a knee again. Two figures burst through the front door, rifles up, and he spun to engage. He nearly fired, but his operator's brain still had enough discipline to recognize the helmets, digital cammies, and coyote-grey body armor as belonging to two United States Marines.

He lowered his pistol as the tense voice finally registered in his ears.

"I say again, Choctaw One—SITREP? What's your status, bro? The Marines are there."

Kemper squeezed his eyes shut tightly and answered. "Bin Jabbar went out the back." His voice sounded like someone had stuffed cotton in his ears. "Don't let him get away."

"Jesus, that's a lot of blood," a young voice said on his right. "Is that all from him?"

He felt hands tighten on his lacerated arm, pressing hard; it burned like someone had just splashed acid on him.

"I'm good, bro," he choked to the Marine beside him. "Go get Bin Jabbar."

"Just gonna get a tourniquet on this arm before you die, dude," the Marine said calmly.

Kemper let himself be forced down to a sitting position on the ground. New and different pain flared just below his left armpit as the Marine applied a tourniquet.

His head felt super swimmy now.

"Good lord," someone said from the doorway. "Did this dude kill all six of these assholes by himself?"

"Someone give me my rifle," Kemper managed to grunt.

The Marines hoisted him to his feet.

He turned to the Marine clutching him under his left armpit and growled at him again. "Rifle, dude."

I'm not going anywhere without my rifle . . .

Someone slipped his SOPMOD M4 into his right hand and he felt other hands dropping his Sig into his holster.

Black fuzz danced in the corners of his eyes and his legs went to jelly as the Marines dragged him through the door to the Humvee waiting in the alley.

Scars: John Dempsey

CHAPTER 6

Al Asad Airbase
Anbar Province, Iraq
June 5
0945 Local Time

Kemper fought back a wave of nausea—which he assumed to be related to the pain medicine they had given him—and stared at the ceiling of the recovery room, which looked more like a plywood warehouse. Gratefully, the field hospital was mostly empty at the moment. Despite how badly his guts churned, he felt nothing in his mutilated left arm.

He'd refused anesthesia, of course, and so they had instead given him what the Navy surgeon assigned to the Marines as part of the Forward Resuscitative Surgical System had called a regional block. The nerve block had made his arm go completely to sleep after a painful injection of medicine just above his left collarbone. The first doc he'd seen had insisted Kemper allow them to put him to sleep—which had almost earned the doc a fist to the jaw. The FRSS surgeon had arrived just in time to keep Kemper from walking out of the pre-op area and hiking back to the Tier One compound. So, he was awake, but his left arm would be useless until the medicine wore off in, like, twelve hours.

"What is your name and unit?" a young woman dressed in Marine cammies and a green T-shirt asked from the foot of his bed. She wore a stethoscope around her neck but looked confused as she flipped through a paper chart that, Kemper knew, had a lot of blanks on it. She looked up from the chart at him—studying her longhaired, bearded patient dressed in unmarked cargo pants and a recently-made-sleeveless black T-shirt. She clearly understood he was not a Marine—and perhaps questioned whether he was in the military at all from his appearance.

"Jack Jones," Kemper said. The "Jones Rule" was one every Tier One SEAL learned during their deployment brief. If asked, give your real first name plus Jones. That was how covert the Tier One activities were. "I'm with a Joint Task Force."

"A 'Joint Task Force'?" she said. "I'm sorry, what unit is that? Where are you based?"

"I'll take care of this, Petty Officer Stancil," said a man walking up behind her. Kemper shifted his gaze to the new arrival—it was the first surgeon who'd treated him . . . the one he'd thought he might have to punch. His uniform identified him as Navy Commander Sharpe. The dismissed medic nodded and shrugged, placed the clipboard on the bed, and headed off. "How's your pain, Mr. Jones?" the surgeon asked, having apparently gotten the standard vague and partial read-in that was protocol when the Tier One unit needed to interact with folks outside its mission.

"No pain, Doc," Kemper said. "Sorry about before."

Sharpe raised a hand and shooed the apology away, but his expression couldn't hide the fact that he'd been waiting for it.

"All good, son," he said. "That was a nasty injury, but the surgeon you guys travel with did a great job. I scrubbed in to assist him, but he apparently is no longer around, so let's tell you what we did." Sharpe leaned on the rail of the bed, all doctor now. "The top part of this wound, here, just below your elbow"—he indicated the spot on Kemper's good arm—"was deep, all the way to the bone. In fact, we could see a groove in the bone where the blade cut into it. You had an injury to the ulnar artery, which we ligated—in other words, we just tied the artery off—because you have a redundant system down that low and the radial artery on the other side was uninjured."

"Will that mess me up?" Kemper asked, concerned. Tying off an artery seemed like a big deal.

"Nah," Sharpe said. "You'll never notice the difference. There are communications between the two arteries all up and down your forearm, so you'll get all the blood supply you need everywhere you need it. Almost miraculously, there was no nerve injury at all. You had considerable damage to the muscles up top, but the wound wrapped around your arm before it got to all those tendons in the lower part of your forearm, so no tendon repair was required at all. The rest of it was just the tedium of sewing everything back together."

"So, good to go, then?" Kemper said, sitting up. He needed to get out of there and see how everyone else was.

"Well, I mean, yeah, but you know—you have some recovery time here. We had to put a lot of stuff back together, and it'll take time to heal. Then you'll need some physical therapy to get your strength back and get you back to normal function. The good news is that you'll have a full recovery, but you'll be doing it back home with your family for now."

Back home? What the hell was this guy talking about? He was about to object when a familiar voice called his attention to the doorway at the end of the room.

"How's he behaving, Doc?" Thiel asked as he approached, hands shoved into his pockets and the sleeves of his "Bars of Virginia Beach" long-sleeve tee bunched up over his thick forearms, tattoos wrapped around both.

"Mysteriously," Sharpe said, shaking his head with a smile. "Excuse me," the doc said and gave them the room.

"Dude, how's Davidson?" Kemper asked.

"Gonna be okay, bro," Thiel answered, "but it was bad. They stabilized him in Ramadi and then sent him to the cache in Balad. Said he needed a vascular surgeon or something, and that's where they have one. Then to Germany, then home, I assume."

Kemper clenched his jaw and nodded. "Everyone else good?"

"Yeah," his friend said. "TBI protocol on Romeo 'cause he whacked his head in the explosion, but he's good. Already being an asshole, so back to normal." They both laughed. "Stitched up some little cut on my scalp back at our compound. Most guys got bumps and bruises. I think Epperson either broke his ankle or sprained it bad, but he's in the med shop with a TENS unit, refusing to get an X-ray. Perry's gonna make him, though, so we'll see." Thiel shifted his gaze to the bulky bandage on Kemper's arm. "And you?"

"Five by, brother," Kemper said. "Just a little PT and I'm back in the saddle. Should be able to do that here and be operational in no time." He looked up at Thiel and gave him a smile he hoped looked genuine. "We still got some ass to kick." For a moment, he saw Bin Jabbar's face laughing at him in the second when he realized he'd fucked up. He needed to be here—with his brothers—to make up for that mistake.

"Thought I heard the doc say you were headed home," Thiel said, his expression going dubious.

"Ahhhh," Kemper said, waving the arm that worked toward the door. "He ain't from NSW, bro. He's not used to working with Team guys."

"Hooyah to that," Thiel said. "When you're done lying around, I got wheels. We can head to the chow hall down by the MWR—the one with the burger bar."

"I missed breakfast?"

"Yeah, bro. It's, like, almost lunch."

"All right," Kemper said. "Get me the fuck out of here."

Thiel pursed his lips. "Mercer wants to talk to you first," the SEAL said. "Gonna be here in a minute. He rode down with me, and I think he's getting a brief from the docs right now on you and Davidson both."

Kemper's stomach sank.

Time to pay the piper.

"Okay," he said, trying to look nonchalant. "Is he pissed about something?"

Thiel lowered his head and raised both his eyebrows. "Dude, are you serious?" He looked over his shoulder and around the long room to make sure they were still alone. "That was some crazy shit, bro. What were you doing? Sprinting around Ramadi like you're fucking Batman. What the hell, man?"

Kemper forced confused indignation onto his face. "'I will draw on every remaining ounce of strength to protect my teammates and complete my mission,'" he said, quoting the SEAL creed.

Thiel shook his head. "Don't give me that shit, Kemp. That was some rogue-ass vigilante shit, bro. That ain't gonna fly in the Teams—not even at the Tier One."

Kemper sighed. "So he's pissed?"

Thiel snorted. "You might want to lead with 'Sir, that will never happen again . . .'"

Kemper gritted his teeth and thought hard about how he was going to save his career.

CHAPTER 7

Al Asad Airbase
Anbar Province, Iraq
June 5
1010 Local Time

Kelso Jarvis kicked the door of the white Toyota Hilux closed with a booted foot and headed for the double doors of the low building that the Marines had converted into a Level II field surgical hospital, his mind on the SEAL inside. Hours ago, he'd watched the infrared silhouette of his newest Tier One SEAL squad leader with mixed feelings. Kemper's rash decision to pursue Bin Jabbar seemed an obvious and serious breach, worthy of serious consequences. Jarvis knew the importance of teamwork and "team before self" as well as, or even better than, anyone, and he'd tossed men out of the Tier One for less egregious offenses.

But there was something about this Jack Kemper.

He ran over again in his head what he'd seen on the feed. Kemper had conducted the assault flawlessly at the beginning. When things took a terrible turn, he'd kept his tactical priorities, secured the building against remaining fighters and any who might join, checked on the other half of his team at the rear, prioritized security and CASEVAC, then coordinated with the TOC and with the perimeter Marines as he pursued the target who had slipped away.

I will protect my teammates and complete my mission.

Where had Kemper broken the promise demanded by the SEAL creed, really?

What hung with him, though, was the ruse—generated on the fly while surrounded by seven men bent on his death. In that moment, Kemper had thought to spin a tale, to calmly convince Bin Jabbar he was the front man of an overwhelming force. The gambit hadn't worked, but it had been brilliant. Still, even that wasn't what had impressed Jarvis. His amazement had come from the cool, calm, confident delivery of the lie—like a seasoned undercover operator working in a NOC.

Jarvis pushed through the left side of the double wooden doors leading to the foyer of the building occupied by the Marine Expeditionary Forces medical support battalion. Only he and a few others in the Tier One ever wore marked uniforms, and this was such a time. As a result, Marines and Sailors from the FSSG looked up to the rare sight of an O-6 with a trident on his chest strolling through their space. Many of them straightened up, nearly to attention, and he walked through a cloud of "Good morning, sirs," requiring him to at least grunt a reply.

"Skipper?"

He turned to see Lieutenant Commander Mercer just inside an office, talking to one of the senior officers from the Shock Trauma Platoon.

"Just checking on our boy, Neal," Jarvis said.

"Yeah," Mercer said with a tone that suggested Kemper's wounds should be the least of the new Tier One SEAL's worries. "Well, the doc here says Kemper was lucky. Lots of muscle damage that will heal quickly, but no significant tendon damage, no long-term problems for the one artery that got damaged, and no nerve damage. He'll head from here to Germany, then to Virginia Beach, and back to Tampa for intensive PT for a few months. Full recovery is the prediction. I intend to be sure he recovers less quickly from the wounds I'm about to inflict." The SEAL officer wore a sour face. "Any thoughts you have before I rip him a new asshole and assign him to administrative duties pending transfer?" Mercer added as a courtesy.

Jarvis knew it wasn't really a question. Clearly, Mercer felt punishment was a no-brainer. And perhaps it should be, but there was something else here.

Something about this Kemper...

It would be trite to think it was because Kemper reminded him of himself. He didn't really, though there were some similarities perhaps.

"Why don't you let me talk to him first, Neal," Jarvis said. "Then I can share my thoughts and he will be all yours. Fair?"

"Perfectly, sir," Mercer said, but his tone indicated confusion. The situation seemed pretty black-and-white to the squadron commander, and that meant Jarvis would have to sell this guy on keeping Kemper if that was the decision. He couldn't have the boss not believing in one of his leaders, for sure.

"Something I'm missing, boss?" Mercer added.

"Maybe," Jarvis admitted. "I'm not sure yet. Let me talk to him."

Mercer nodded, and Jarvis headed to the double doors of the recovery area.

Maybe thoughts of the whole new world he was preparing himself for were biasing him about Kemper. There would be no black-and-white in the murky grey world of the new task force he would be standing up next year, after the "retirement" from the Navy that had not yet been announced. The

Joint Intelligence Research Group would be the super-secret tool this war on terror needed, and there, he would need men who could live in the middle of that murky grey view of the world. With a little more time, Kemper might just be one of those men.

He nodded to a cammie-clad doctor with "Sharpe" on his name tape. "Commander Sharpe," he said in greeting. "Okay to talk to my guy?"

"Yes, sir. Of course," the surgeon said. "Only patient in there right now."

Jarvis pushed through the swinging doors and saw Kemper in the lone occupied bed, arguing with the poor girl beside him.

"What I'm saying is, I'm leaving shortly and I don't need this damn IV. I'm hydrated, for crying out loud. And I have to pee—again. I want my IV out and I'm going to the head. I'm not peeing in your friggin' thermos again."

Jarvis shook his head as he approached. At least it sounded like Kemper was trying to clean up his salty SEAL language for the poor girl he was arguing with.

"And I told you, they said you're headed to Germany, and you can't travel on the medical flight without an IV. I'm just doing my job, and you're making it harder than it should be."

"Maybe I can help," Jarvis said, his voice the rough gravel of the SEAL legend persona he knew his men needed him to be. Always, he had a sixth sense that allowed him to know just which of his myriad personas any situation or group needed.

"Sir," Kemper said, sitting up straighter in the bed.

"Stop being an asshole, Mr. Jones," Jarvis growled.

"Yes, sir," Kemper said, then turned to the young medic. "My apologies," he added, a child forced to make nice on the playground.

"Give us the room, Petty Officer," Jarvis said to the medic.

"Gladly, sir," the woman said, making no attempt to hide that she'd had enough of Kemper.

Standing beside Kemper's bed with his hands clasped behind his back, Jarvis watched her leave. When the doors swung back closed, he turned to his SEAL.

"Wanna tell me what happened, Jack?" he asked, his tone softer now.

"Sir?" The SEAL seemed surprised by the use of his first name, but also—wisely—seemed to be treading carefully, like he was walking through a minefield.

Which he is . . .

Jarvis pursed his lips and nodded. "So, listen to me, Jack. You may be at a crossroads here, careerwise, son. Mercer wants your ass on a spit, and I'm deciding whether to give it to him or not. You'll want to be more honest than cautious here. We're gonna chat a moment, you'll tell me where your head was during the various decision points on this operation, and then we'll decide what happens next. Clear?"

"Clear, sir," Kemper replied, his voice tight.

"Problem with any of that?"

Kemper sighed, resigned, perhaps. "None, sir."

"Walk me through it, frogman."

Kemper did, starting with the infil and how they'd approached the breach. He walked through the breach, the clearing of the room, engaging the fighters upstairs, and the explosion as the second element breached the rear gate. He walked through the securing of the stairs, moving to the rear, checking the team status, arranging the Marines to collapse in and provide both security and CASEVAC. Then he paused.

"So, obviously, this is the decision we're most interested in, Mr. Kemper. At this point you pursued the HVT and two others through the streets of Ramadi, doubtless surrounded by enemy fighters, by your fucking self."

"Yes, sir," Kemper said. He no longer seemed nervous, or even resigned, but confident. A fire burned in those dark eyes. "We had received casualties, but I'd arranged for their security and exfil. Taking a swim buddy with me seemed like it would only further jeopardize my teammates and add little to my situation. It was my hope to line up a shot as I turned the corner—where I would not even be out of a sightline from the rear element of my team. The fact that the targets had disappeared already suggested to me that they could not have gone far. With Variable in my ear—and you, as well, sir—I elected to attempt to complete the mission if the target was still within the block."

"By yourself?"

"I collapsed the second line of security from the 3/8 into my position for fire support and exfil, sir."

"You didn't make that call until you had already decided to breach the room, where you confronted seven heavily armed fighters by yourself."

"Until I had information on my situation, it didn't seem prudent to pull the 3/8 Marines through insurgent-rich streets—putting them in harm's way—until I knew I would need them."

Jarvis let the long pause hang in the air, giving the impression he was carefully considering the information he'd received.

He didn't need to consider it, actually. He knew what he would do.

"After which you single-handedly killed six of the seven insurgents, sustaining a significant injury in the process, and the HVT escaped."

"Regrettably, sir."

Jarvis sighed this time. "If you were confronted with the same situation again, Petty Officer Kemper, would you make the same decision?"

Kemper seemed to struggle a moment, but then looked up and held Jarvis's eyes.

"Without the benefit of hindsight—yes, sir," he said.

The SEAL's voice had changed. Clearly Kemper felt confident, but there was something else—a fire that *did* remind Jarvis of himself. Of the young SEAL he'd once been—but perhaps also of the mission focused man he'd become.

"I saw an opportunity to complete the mission against a high-value target—a target we'd briefed was crucial to not only turning the tide in the upcoming offensive in Ramadi, but also in what will likely be the next big phase of the war here, out west near Al Qa'im and the Syrian border—and decided that outweighed the risk. My team was secure and the CASEVAC and exfil were underway, and this seemed the best move." He paused. "Next time, I would probably task one shooter to go with me as swim buddy, but at the time, it seemed the rear element needed to be together, and I judged it would take too long to pull Perry or Sandman from the front. I might change that decision, faced with the same scenario again."

Jarvis paced, careful to keep his face a mask as he thought about what Kemper had said. This SEAL was not the door-kicking, black-and-white, mission-focused Team guy he imagined himself to be. He had weighed long-term strategic priorities in his decision, seemingly without being aware he had done so.

This is a SEAL the Tier One needs now and that my next task force will need someday.

But first, he needed to be reined in.

Kemper seemed to sense the hesitation, and jumped on it.

"Sir, they want to send me to Germany. I need to stay with the Team. I can rehab in garrison and be back in the fight when ready, but long before this deployment is over. Going home makes no sense, and will only add to the stress on my family that this assignment is already having."

"There is talk of sending you farther away than just home, Jack," Jarvis said, but kept some of the edge out of his voice now. He paced to the foot of the bed and stared at the wounded SEAL with hard eyes. "There's no room for a fucking Rambo in real life—not in the Teams and especially not in this, the premier JSOC unit. We can make a real impact only when groups of warriors work together, complementing one another's strengths and weaknesses. We function best as a collective, and when one operator goes rogue, it not only lessens mission success, it puts lives in danger. Hell, it's why we do the ridiculous log PT in BUD/S, to show, from the very beginning, that you accomplish nothing alone and succeed only as a team. Team before self, Mr. Kemper. Any of that sound familiar?"

"Yes, sir," Kemper said, but his eyes suggested the SEAL didn't think he had violated those principles—other than by kicking in the door himself. "I agree with that, sir, and my brothers are my life. But stopping this asshole here meant preventing another dangerous mission later. We were tasked with a mission—"

Jarvis held up a hand, cutting him off.

"Mr. Kemper, I'm inclined to give you a second chance to prove I'm not wrong about you. I'll discuss this with Lieutenant Commander Mercer, but I intend to recommend this be a life lesson we let you prove you've learned from. But if you show me I've made a mistake, Jack"—he leaned in now, hands on the bed rail—"I will fuck you beyond your ability to imagine. Are we clear?"

"Clear, sir," Kemper said, relief in his eyes. "About going home, though, sir, I—"

Jarvis let out a barking laugh. "You can't seriously think you're in a position to make demands."

"No, sir," Kemper said, looking at his hands—one just fingers sticking out of a bulky dressing. "But if I don't reengage with this team until they return from this deployment—"

"Enough," Jarvis said, cutting him off again. "Here's what we'll do. You stop being an asshole to the medical staff here.

You go to Germany and begin PT there. If they clear you for self-driven PT in a few weeks, then you'll return to the squadron here in Al Asad and work the TOC until the JSOC surgeons clear you for duty. In that time, you will commit to seeing the big picture of these operations, and then take that perspective with you into the field. You'll work with the N2 and JSOC J2 to see the big picture in the intelligence analysis during the day, and help run the TOC at night. Questions?"

"None, sir," Kemper said, the fire back. "And thank you, sir."

"Don't thank me yet, Jack," Jarvis said and laughed. "Mercer is still going to want a piece of your ass."

"He can have it, sir," Kemper responded immediately. "That young medic out there will confirm I have plenty of ass to go around."

"All right, then," Jarvis said. "I'll have Thiel pull together a bag for your trip to Germany." He stuck out his right hand and the SEAL shook it firmly. "I have a long memory, Jack. One day, you'll owe me for this."

"You won't regret it, sir," Kemper predicted. "And I'll follow you anywhere you ask me to go, sir. Anywhere, anytime."

Jarvis spun on a heel, keeping his smile to himself.

He intended to collect on that one day.

But for now, he had to figure out a way to sell this to Mercer—and somehow let the superb SEAL officer believe it was his idea.

CHAPTER 8

Al Asad Airbase
Anbar Province, Iraq
Five weeks later

As he felt the C-130 turn to taxi, Kemper rhythmically squeezed a rubber ball in his left hand. Each squeeze brought pain, tearing from below at the angry red wound that wrapped his forearm. But the pain was background noise, a futile protest of the flesh against the iron will pounding with his heartbeat. The muscles inside his forearm—where absorbable sutures still held the tissues together—could scream all they wanted. He was a SEAL, damn it, and his body was a servant to his mind. He transformed the pain into heavy metal music in his mind and PT'd to the rhythm.

Squeeze . . . squeeze . . . squeeze . . .

Leaning forward, he looked out the round window into the darkness and toward the red lights on the south side of the runway. As he squeezed, he let the fingertips of his right hand probe the thick red scar where the jihadist's dagger had cut him to the bone. In time, the angry serpentine scar would soften . . . bleach pearly white from sea and sun and time. But for now, it called for attention—advertising loudly to all the world his mistake in Ramadi.

"Know where you're going?" someone asked from behind him, and he turned to see an Air Force loadmaster beside him, a long cord stretching from his helmet to the bulkhead farther forward. "You're not with those guys, right?" he asked, gesturing with his head to the group of two dozen clean-cut military members in Marine digital cammies marked with Navy insignia.

"No," Kemper replied, smiling. "Not with them."

The crewman nodded, looking him up and down, taking in the thick beard, the backwards ball cap, and the unmarked clothes.

"Didn't think so," he said and smiled back. "Got someone meeting you?"

"Yeah," he said. "All squared away. Thanks for the lift."

The Air Force man nodded and headed aft to talk to the other passengers—Navy support personnel for the Marines here, Kemper guessed, turning back to the window. Outside, he spotted a white Toyota Hilux near the fence line, Thiel sitting on the hood.

He'd kept in the loop on the SIPRNET the last few weeks, so he knew taking out Zarqawi would no longer be his honor. Nor had it been tasking for his brothers in the Tier One. The terrorist had bought it from a precision bomb just a couple of days after their op, dropped on his head after tireless work from OGA and military intelligence professionals squeezing their assets in Ramadi. That had done nothing to curb the violence, however. Power abhors a vacuum, and the death of Zarqawi had come before the 3/8 Marines gained control of the city center and set up combat outposts throughout the city. If anything, the sectarian violence had surged after the assassination, and the new, fractured leaders of the insurgency in Ramadi were killing more people than ever.

Kemper squeezed the ball harder and harder, remembering Alan from SEAL Team Three telling him about the insurgents executing children—their bodies hung from walls as warnings to other who might help the Americans—and he gritted his teeth. He needed to get back in the saddle as soon as possible, because the sporadic attacks on Americans in outposts in Ramadi were only increasing and becoming deadlier. Whatever jihadis were leading the violence in Ramadi needed to meet with some frogman justice.

He intended to be part of that justice as soon as possible.

Squeeze . . . squeeze . . . squeeze . . .

A loud pop made the sailors clad in Marine cammies jump in unison, like one single organism, and stare at Kemper.

"Sorry," he called out, holding the remnants of the rubber ball up as an explanation.

If my arm's good enough to pop a fucking rubber ball, I should be good to get back in the fight

He gathered up his gear—just an oversized backpack, since all his other gear and weapons were still on the JSOC compound—and headed to the rear of the plane, smiling sheepishly at the sailors, who regarded him with curious fascination. Several months into his deployment beard, Kemper imagined himself looking quite the sight. The cargo plane lurched to a halt, but the sailors remained, seat belts in place, perhaps expecting a flight attendant to announce they had arrived at the gate.

Kemper chuckled to himself as the rear ramp began to lower. He waited next to the helmeted crewman standing at the break, controlling the ramp's descent. As the ramp approached the ground, Kemper stepped onto the still-descending platform and nodded to the Air Force loadmaster.

"Thanks again, bro," he said.

"Happy hunting, dude," the man said, shooting a thumbs-up.

He'd hauled enough people, this guy, that he knew when he saw a warrior, Kemper supposed. You could keep your uniform slick, but an operator looked like an operator, however you dressed him up.

Thiel slid off the hood of the pickup and wrapped him in a bear hug as he approached the Hilux. "How's the arm, bro?"

"Five by, brother," Kemper replied, the circle of fire from his rumination still bright around him. "You guys gettin' some?"

Thiel grinned. "Yeah, bro," he said and slipped into the driver's seat as Kemper tossed his backpack into the bed of the truck. "And then some. We have a nice stream of intel working, and we're kicking some serious ass. We've operated twenty-eight of the last thirty days, killed I don't know how many shitheads, and have pulled fourteen intelligence-rich HVTs off X's all over western Iraq."

"Are we evening the score in Ramadi?" Kemper asked, slipping into the passenger seat.

Thiel looked at him as he started the truck by flipping an ignition switch instead of using a key. His face seemed genuinely confused, but Kemper got it immediately. After he'd left, they'd continued to prosecute targets over and over, while all he'd had to process in his mind, night after night, was his failure in Ramadi.

"Nah, bro," Thiel said. "Nothing of strategic value in Ramadi right now. We pulled one of Zarqawi's lieutenants out of a shithole goat farm west of the glass factory a few weeks ago, but that's the last time we've been there. Team Three is doing some righteous shit out there, but it's not JSOC Tier targets for now."

Kemper nodded and said nothing, unsure why a funk hung over him at this news. They were the Tier One, the instrument of justice and strategic badassery for JSOC. Ramadi was a white-side war now.

He looked out the window as they drove around the south edge of the flight line, lights out, following the red lights beside the perimeter road toward their little chain-link-fence-secured compound. The sun teased the horizon with a splash of light, the sky responded with a purple-toned pout, and Kemper looked at his watch. He could use a few minutes before facing the rest of the gang inside the compound.

"Grab some breakfast before we head back?" he asked. "That little Pakistani dude will be firing up the made-to-order omelet station about now," he added, knowing from a prior deployment that those omelets were Thiel's weak spot.

And sure enough, his teammate grimaced and then smiled in anticipation. "We'll grab the guys, then head down," he said.

Kemper nodded, but would have preferred this first meal to be just the two of them. He had no idea what the rest of the team thought about his actions in Ramadi that night a month ago, but it would have been nice to get a temperature reading from Thiel before finding out the hard way.

"Cool," he said.

"First," Thiel said, his expression suggesting he hoped to get information from Kemper rather than convey it, "the CSO is back in country and wants to meet you privately for some reason. What's that about, Jack?"

Kemper shrugged, but felt his pulse tick up at the news. Jarvis had said Kemper owed him, but it seemed a little early to collect. Maybe the boss simply wanted to check on his investment.

"No idea," he said. "He had my back, I can tell you that, but I've not had any contact with him while in Germany. Shit, you and Perry are the only ones that checked in regularly. I got a few obscene messages from Romeo and Sandman, but that's it. I got no idea what the boss man wants. I didn't even know Jarvis was back playing in the sandbox."

Thiel nodded. "No one did—hell, no one does. He asked me to drop you here at the gate, then wait for you while he takes you somewhere. He's acting all spooky and shit. Guess I thought you might read me in."

"I would if I knew anything, bro," Kemper said, his curiosity now more than piqued. "But I got no idea."

They took the short access road, then bore left, following the road that led to the JSOC compound and little else. Outside and left of the two gates, another Hilux sat idling with the lights out, as light discipline demanded on the base even now—five years into the war.

"See you when you get back, Jack," Thiel said, putting the Hilux in park. "Maybe you can tell me what the hell is going on."

"Maybe," Kemper said with a smile, getting out of the truck, then closing the door and leaning in through the open passenger side window. "See you in a minute?"

"He said he needed less that twenty," Thiel replied.

Kemper left his backpack in the rear of Thiel's Hilux, opened the passenger side door to the other truck, and slid in.

"Hey, Jack," Jarvis said. He was dressed in 5.11 Tactical cargo pants and a plaid, short-sleeved Oakley shirt. The CSO grinned at him as he put the truck in drive and pulled away, passing by the compound and heading east along the dark perimeter road. "Sorry to be so mysterious, son, but I thought there was someone you might like to meet. Not everyone in the unit is read in on this—in fact, I can count them on one hand. I figured I'd grab you before you check in. Hope you don't mind."

Kemper shook his head, completely confused.

Not everyone is read in? Then why grab me? I'm just an E-6 squad leader...

Kemper felt suddenly very uncomfortable. He had no idea what to say to the legendary SEAL driving him around the dark flight line, so he said nothing.

Just before the easternmost approach end of the main runway, Jarvis pulled the truck off the pavement and onto a dirt road. After about two hundred yards, the road descended below a berm, and Kemper spied a small cabin-style building beside a fuel depot he'd never noticed before. Jarvis pulled up to a gate where a man, fully kitted up in black gear over blue jeans and a grey T-shirt, stepped up to the driver's side window.

"Oh hey, Captain Jarvis. They said you were coming. Head right in."

The man pulled a heavy gate aside, then closed it behind them as Jarvis drove the truck into a small lot with three other identical Hilux pickups. He parked the truck and turned to smile at Kemper.

"You ready for this, Jack?"

"For what, exactly, sir?" Kemper asked.

Jarvis turned further in his seat, the sinewy muscles in his forearms rippling in the moonlight as he gripped the steering wheel.

"The thing about our world, Jack, is that every time you think you've made it, that you're at the highest security level, the most read-in on the badass assignments in our super-secret-squirrel-shit community, you eventually come to realize that there is *always* another level above you. You know what I mean?"

"I think so, sir," he said.

"Jack, I'm not reading you in on what's going on here, okay?"

Kemper nodded.

"But I want you to remember how it felt when you saw what I'm about to show you. And one day, when I reach out to you in the future, remember this feeling and know there is always, always a bigger fish to fry. Got it?"

"Got it, sir," Kemper replied, but he was almost certain that he did not.

Jarvis climbed out of the truck, and Kemper followed him to a stucco building with a heavy iron door, sitting alone in the middle of a concertina-wire-topped square of twelve-foot fencing. He watched Jarvis press his palm to a black tablet beside the door, which turned green and lit up a red keyboard. Jarvis entered a series of numbers while Kemper forced himself to look away for some reason. A magnetic lock clicked open and the door hissed cool air, licking the dry heat from his face.

Jarvis pulled the door open.

There was no foyer, just a short, dark hallway ending in an elevator. Kemper stopped at the elevator and Jarvis punched in a new code, and a single door slid open. Inside the elevator car, the SEAL Captain pressed the lower of the two unmarked buttons. The elevator door slid shut and the car descended. Kemper had no idea how far, but based on the perceived speed and time that elapsed, it was no short distance. At the bottom, the door slid open, revealing what could easily be mistaken for the bullpen of a major metropolitan newspaper—numerous cubicles filled with men and women working at computers or talking across the thin dividers that separated them.

"How are you, Captain Jarvis?" a woman asked from the closest cubicle.

"Here to see your guy," Jarvis said.

"Yes, sir," the woman said. "Mr. Reynolds said you'd be stopping by. Anything you need?"

"No, thank you, Mary," Jarvis said. As they walked around the cluster of cubicles, Jarvis said, "That was Mary Jones," as if that would explain everything—and Kemper supposed it did explain a lot. No doubt everyone in this place was a Jones.

Jarvis led him to another metal security door and entered yet another passcode.

The door clicked and then hissed open, and he followed Jarvis inside.

This hallway, or tunnel rather, felt completely different from the room they'd just left. For starters, it was constructed of stone and concrete. Not only was it dark, it was also wet, and the air had an unpleasant metallic odor. On both sides of the tunnel, small cells—for lack of a better term—had been carved into the rock itself, three to a side and covered with two-inch thick Plexiglas etched with holes, presumably for airflow. Kemper was reminded of the movie about the serial killer helping the female FBI agent. The first two cells on the right held sleeping prisoners in orange jumpsuits, but Jarvis passed them by, stopping and turning in front of the last cell on the left.

Inside, a thin man sat cross-legged on the floor as if meditating, eyes closed and hands in his lap, but his lips moving, perhaps in prayer or perhaps something else. Kemper recognized the man immediately, despite the oily hair pasted to his forehead and the large bruises distorting one side of his face. Kemper's pulse quickened and the world seemed to tilt, as if he'd just slid down a rabbit hole into a place more bizarre than Wonderland.

"My God," he breathed. "It's really him."

"Yep," Jarvis said simply.

On the floor of the cavelike cell sat Abu Musab al-Zarqawi—the terrorist and jihadist who'd owned Ramadi. Killer of scores of Americans, responsible for the beheading of American journalist Nick Berg, and later that same year, American civilian Owen Armstrong, both of whom had died while Kemper fought with SEAL Team Eight. This man had been linked to more than seven hundred deaths during the initial invasion in 2003 and thousands more since. An evil sociopath, leading other evil sociopaths, and here he sat, in some super-secret dark hole not a half mile from the JSOC Tier One compound.

"I thought he was killed in an air strike a few days after our operation against Bin Jabbar."

"Yes," Jarvis said. He turned and held Kemper's eyes. "Simpler that way, don't you think?"

Kemper shook his head, trying to shake off the eerie, otherworldly feeling that enveloped him. "I suppose so, sir," he said.

Just then, the terrorist's eyes snapped open, like a vampire released from a trance, and Kemper felt himself start. The man held his eyes, a queer smile spreading over his face; it gave Kemper a shudder like he'd just been plunged into cold water.

Jarvis gestured with his head, and Kemper followed him back up the hall, stopping just at the door.

"I'm sorry, sir. Why . . . ?"

Jarvis nodded. "Why show you? First, understand you will violate every law concerning access to classified materials you've ever signed and promised to protect if you share a word of this with anyone."

Kemper nodded. *Who the fuck would even believe him?*

"I showed you this for two reasons, Jack. First, to show you that what we do at the Tier One matters. When we cap some shithead, or pull some HVT or material off the X, we don't often get to fully know what fruits are born of our labor. I wanted you to know that there is, indeed, great fruit. Second, I want you to remember that there is always a bigger fish."

Jarvis held his eyes now, telling him something, but Kemper was unsure what.

"Understood, sir," he said anyway.

"Jack, there are only a handful of men who can function in the world of the Tier One units," Jarvis continued. "But far fewer still are prepared or qualified to take a trip down the bunny hole to the real heart of how we keep America safe. I showed you this because I believe, in time, you may well be such a man."

Kemper stared at his boss, at the legend who had awed him for years, and felt a new level of almost reverence embrace him.

Kelso Jarvis is the fucking man.

"I'm going to ask you to focus with full effort, beyond any distraction, on the task of being the best damn Tier One SEAL the unit has ever had. I have cleared the obstacles created by what happened in Ramadi for you, and I expect you to rise in leadership quickly in this unit. And one day"—he put a paternal hand on Kemper's shoulder—"I may come to you and ask you to do even more."

Kemper nodded. The weight of what Jarvis had said felt real, but not oppressive, not a burden. It felt more like a privilege—perhaps even an honor. Kemper believed, deeply and with all his being, in the experiment of United States democracy and took seriously his promise to protect her and her citizens. What Jarvis was suggesting seemed like only the next natural extension of that promise.

"I understand, sir," he said, the gravity of the moment fully sunk in.

"I know you do, son," Jarvis said. Then he smiled. "Let's get you to breakfast with your team. There's work for them tonight. You'll be in the TOC with me, like we agreed. There, you'll study, learn, and absorb. And one day, a few years from now, I will come calling to collect on your promise."

Before Kemper could answer, the SEAL officer pulled open the heavy door and led him out of the dark, dank underbelly of the War on Terror.

Kemper followed, tracing his fingertip along the serpentine scar that would forever decorate his left arm. Like all scars, it was a visible reminder of a painful event that could not be undone . . . a mistake he could not forget. His scar was born from hubris and passion, from courage and naïveté. And yet as much as he wanted to hate it, to hide the omnipresent reminder of his failure and shame, it also represented something else. Something transformational. In earning this scar, he had earned Captain Jarvis's attention and respect. In earning this scar, he had gained a mentor and been invited to participate in a world previously hidden to him.

His gaze went to the SEAL walking in front of him.

Powerful words materialized in his mind: *I will follow this man wherever he leads, carry whatever burden he asks, and when the day comes and he calls on me to repay my debt, I will answer the call . . . no matter the price.*

THE END

JACK KEMPER WILL RETURN AS JOHN DEMPSEY IN

COLLATERAL
BOOK SIX IN THE TIER ONE SERIES

ON SALE SEPTEMBER 1, 2020

READ ON FOR A SNEAK PEEK

CHAPTER 1

The Ferry House English Pub
London, England
September 14
2147 Local Time

John Dempsey ducked just before the bottle flying at him could slam into his temple. It sailed over his head instead and smashed into a life-sized ceramic English bulldog positioned just inside the pub's entrance. The bottle, and the bulldog, shattered into a million comingled pieces. The barmaid behind the counter released an eardrum-piercing shriek—full of outrage and anguish at the loss of what must have been the pub's mascot.

"Get ooooout!" she screamed. "All of you brigands!"

Nobody listened . . . except for the man Dempsey was there to kill. The Russian operative darted out the pub's double doors, running like a man on fire.

"The target has just left the building," said a professorial voice through the wireless microtransmitter stuffed deep in Dempsey's right ear canal. The voice belonged to Task Force Ember's Signals Chief and Acting Director, Ian Baldwin, located in a Tactical Operations Center five time zones away.

"I know," Dempsey—a former Navy SEAL turned American assassin—said as he blocked a punch from a burly middle-aged local with his forearm. He was about to drive a hook into the guy's jaw but decided the poor bloke didn't deserve to spend the next six weeks drinking all his meals through a straw. So instead, he sent the tough-guy wannabe flying backward and onto his ass with a two-handed shove. He whirled toward the exit to pursue his quarry, only to find another angry brawler blocking his path.

"Dude, where are you?" said another voice, this one belonging to former SEAL and combat surgeon Dan Munn, who was also sitting in the TOC in Florida. "He's getting away."

"I know!" Dempsey growled, ducking a jab flying at his face.

"Well, what the hell are you doing?"

"Somehow Alpha has managed to get himself into a bar fight," came a third voice, this one belonging to Elizabeth Grimes, Ember's sniper in residence and overwatch for tonight's assassination mission.

"Of course he has," Munn said, and Dempsey could practically hear him shaking his head. "Screw this. I say we have Lizzie shoot the target."

"No," came Baldwin's clipped reply. "The DNI was very specific about the approved lethal methods for this operation. No sniper action unless we can disappear the body without incident. Bravo, you are relegated to spotter and exfil activities only."

"Check," Grimes said, acknowledging the directive.

The chatter in Dempsey's ear was beginning to piss him off, and so was the asshole in front of him trying to channel Rocky Balboa. The dude threw a gut punch, which Dempsey caught in a scissor block. The block made the brawler wince, but he was committed and drew back his other fist to try again. Dempsey didn't give him that opportunity; he drove a knee into the man's groin, buckling the wannabe boxer at the waist.

"Behind you," Grimes said in his ear.

Dempsey dropped into a crouch and spun on the balls of his feet. A third dude, the bottle thrower, was charging with a fresh bottle raised overheard and primed to split open Dempsey's skull. Dempsey grabbed him by the shirt, pivoted, and used the attacker's momentum to send him flying into tough guy number two, who was still bent over, clutching his nuts. Both men crashed to the ground in a tangled heap of arms and legs amid a pile of overturned wooden chairs.

Dempsey did a quick scan for the next threat, but there was nobody left standing in the tiny pub. For an instant, he locked eyes with the woman behind the bar. Thank God this was London and not Houston, or else he would be staring down the barrel of a Remington 870. As it was, the only targeting lasers fixed on him at the moment were the invisible ones streaming from her angry eyes.

"Sorry about your bulldog," he said with an Irish brogue as he turned to leave.

"Get the fuck out," she screamed as he barreled out the pub's double doors and onto the street. "And never come back!"

"Which way did he go?" Dempsey asked to the ether, scanning right, then left, for his target.

"North on East Ferry Road," Grimes answered.

"Check," he said and took off after the Russian spy. After one block, the ancient and uneven brick pavers underfoot transitioned to asphalt, improving Dempsey's footing and letting him push to a full tilt. "How are your eyes, Omega?" he asked, noting the misty, overcast night sky.

"We have the target on satellite thermal," Baldwin said. "He has a two-block lead on you and is headed toward Mudchute Park."

"Is that the giant fucking goat farm?"

"Yes, John," Baldwin said, breaking OPSEC as usual. "Mudchute Park and Farm is the largest working farm in London. It's heavily wooded and spans twelve hectares, so I suggest you hurry before you lose him."

"I know, I know. I'm running. I know you can see that," Dempsey puffed.

"Oh, we see you. Is that all you got, old man?" Munn chimed in.

Dempsey didn't answer, preferring to conserve precious oxygen. He hated this shit. Lately, it seemed like every op ended in a foot race—either with him chasing down some fleet-footed asshole, or with him running for his life while being shot at by Russians. Ember didn't need operators; what it needed was Olympic middle-distance runners.

I'm too fucking old for this shit, he thought as his quads began to burn.

"Alpha, this is Bravo," Grimes said in his ear. "I'm coming down. Gonna bring the car around to the east side and reposition on Stebondale Street. If our tango crosses Millwall Park playing fields, I'll plink him with the long gun."

"I said no sniper action," Baldwin said, his voice with an uncharacteristic hard edge. "Accidental death or poison—that was the OPORD."

"We tried poison and that didn't work out so well," Munn said. "So now it's time to try accidental death."

"Enlighten me, Dan, if you will. How does a sniper round to the head qualify as accidental death?" Baldwin said.

"It qualifies when the target *accidentally* walks into Lizzie's bullet while it happens to be flying in the vicinity of his head," the SEAL doc said, oozing with sarcasm.

"OPSEC, people, OPSEC!" snapped an acerbic fourth voice on the line. "I'm good, but so is British Intelligence. GCHQ is listening." The rebuke from Richard Wang, Ember's cyber and IT expert, was as out of character as truth was from a politician.

To Dempsey's surprise, everybody shut up and locked it down.

Thank God . . .

He pulled up a mental image of the nearby greenspace complex, consisting of Millwall Park and Mudchute Farm. He didn't have an eidetic memory, but he'd always had a knack for remembering topography and details from satellite imagery. As a SEAL with the Tier One back in the day, it had been his responsibility to plan the ops and know the terrain cold. Yes, they'd had GPS, Suunto watches, slick tablet computers, and eyes in the sky to monitor their position, but Dempsey knew better than to put all his faith in technology. Because unlike his teammates, technology seemed to have an annoying habit of letting him down when he needed it most.

Mudchute Farm was a genuine anomaly; nothing of the sort existed in American cities. At thirty-two acres, it was huge and situated on the Isle of Dogs, a peninsula inside a buttonhook bow of the Thames in central London, where real estate was going at a premium. More than just a greenspace, the farm had a wooded perimeter, an equestrian center, and grazing pastures for cows, pigs, goats, sheep, and llama. The farm had caught Dempsey's attention not only because of its size, but also because it was the perfect place to disappear or wait in ambush.

"Target is approaching the Chapel House Street intersection," Baldwin reported. "And he just vectored east toward the park."

"Check," Dempsey said.

"And he appears to be opening the gap, Alpha. Can you possibly run any faster?"

"If I... could run... any faster," he said, his words punctuated by heavy exhales, "then I would... be."

"Target is crossing the northwest quadrant... heading for the woods and Mudchute Farm," Munn said. "Bravo, where are you?"

"Driving, but not in position yet," Grimes said. "Ninety seconds."

"Shit, you're gonna be too late," Munn said, as if sniper action were still on the table.

Arms pumping and legs churning, Dempsey crossed the Manchester Grove intersection. In another two hundred meters, he'd reach the park entrance. Two-story brown-brick row houses zipped past him as he sprinted up the middle of Ferry Road between twin columns of parked cars. As he ran, he noted how he could barely feel the formfitting body armor protecting his torso. This was his first time wearing the brand-new tech Baldwin had procured for all the SAD team members.

Unlike traditional antiballistic Kevlar vests with heavy, rigid SAPI plates, this new vest was light and flexible. The puncture-resistant woven shell concealed a honeycomb interior filled with "liquid" body armor. Originally conceived at MIT and then refined by DARPA, liquid body armor—or shear-thickening fluid—was flexible and viscous in normal conditions but instantly hardened when struck by a projectile, deflecting and dispersing the impact force. He'd rolled his eyes and chuckled when Baldwin had presented him with the vest, but after unloading a thirty-round magazine of 5.56 at the range and finding it intact, his skepticism had melted away. Wearing it now, however, he couldn't help but wonder what critical little piece of information Baldwin had "forgotten" to mention.

He could almost hear the Signal Chief's voice in his head.

Antiballistic STF performs flawlessly against all calibers of ammunition . . . so long as it doesn't get wet. Or maybe, *Liquid body armor is positively impenetrable . . . provided the gel temperature stays below ninety-one degrees Fahrenheit.*

He suddenly found himself wishing for his old rigid, heavy, uncomfortable-as-fuck body armor. He'd been shot plenty of times in that rig and had walked away every time.

Well . . . almost every time.

"Target is in the woods," Munn reported, just as Dempsey reached the park entrance.

He hurdled the entry gate and ran a dogleg path left, slowing and looking for cover as he scanned the tree line. His spidey sense was tingling as the risk profile shifted. The Russian was in cover now, and Dempsey was exposed—especially while crossing the field.

"Do you have eyes on my tango?" Dempsey said, panting and dropping into a crouch.

"Hold," came Baldwin's reply. "The target is loitering just inside the tree line four hundred feet from your position."

Dempsey took a knee and pulled a compact Sig Sauer from his underarm holster. Wishing he had night-vision goggles, he scanned the tree line over the new, low-profile SAS fiber-tritium sights. "Bearing?"

"Zero four five, true."

"Check," Dempsey said, verifying his watch compass heading and adjusting his aim right.

"The target is moving," Baldwin said, his voice ripe with tension. "Moving north and east, through the trees."

Dempsey popped up from his crouch and sprinted along the line he'd just been sighting. He crossed a walking path and wove his way into the trees and underbrush.

"Target is out of the woods, crossing what looks like a very large vegetable patch. He's heading for one of the paddocks," Baldwin said.

"I'm on it," Dempsey said, pressing forward through the surprisingly dense undergrowth with a cringeworthy lack of stealth.

"Oh dear..."

"'Oh dear' what?" Dempsey said, his voice low and hushed.

"We lost him."

"How is that even possible?"

"He must suspect we have him on satellite thermal, because he moved in among the animals—sheep, I suspect—and entered a barn-like structure. He must be on all fours, because we cannot identify which heat signature is his."

"Are you telling me you can't tell the difference between a man and a bunch of sheep?" Dempsey said through clenched teeth.

"Dude, he's telling you straight," Munn interjected. "It just looks like a bunch of yellow-orange blobs huddled together."

"Ridiculous," Dempsey murmured and couldn't help but think how he'd gone from being a kitted-up Tier One SEAL, fast-roping with his unit out of Stealth Hawks behind enemy lines, to this . . . a dude stalking sheep in a petting zoo.

In the distance, sirens began to wail.

"There's a police cruiser en route to the Ferry House Pub," Wang reported, his voice all business.

"Time to wrap this up, Alpha," Baldwin said. "You have five minutes to eliminate the target, or I'm terminating the op."

Yeah, yeah, easy for you to say over your tea and biscuits, Dempsey thought as he grudgingly acknowledged Baldwin's order with a double-click of his tongue.

He advanced silently and methodically toward the animal pen where the Russian operative was hiding. The perimeter was kept by a sturdy four-foot-tall slat-and-wire fence with two swing gates. Inside, the turf had been grazed down to bare dirt. A simple, twenty-foot-long windowless shelter with a flat metal roof occupied the south end of the pen. With his pistol trained on the building, he eased along the fence until the opening of the shelter—wide enough to permit free and easy movement in and out by the animals—came into view. The inside of the shelter was pitch black, but he could make out grayish blobs moving just inside the opening.

A second later, the smell hit him and one of the animals let out a throaty, prolonged bleat.

Yep, definitively sheep.

If this were Afghanistan, the tactical solution would be simple—toss a grenade in the barn and hose down everything that came out. But this wasn't the 'Stan. In central London, lobbing grenades and shooting anything, even a bunch of sheep, was off the table. Which meant he had no choice but to go in after his target. And he could predict how that would play out. The minute he entered the barn, commotion would ensue. The animals would bleat and shit and scuttle, and while he milled about trying to find a crouching human in the chaos, his adversary would plink him with an easy headshot.

Dempsey cursed to himself, trying to decide what the hell to do.

"What is the problem, Alpha?" Baldwin said, his tone more annoyed than concerned.

"He's trying to figure out how to get the sheep out of the barn without discharging his weapon," Munn answered for Dempsey.

"Ah yes, do be careful not to kill any sheep, John," Baldwin said. "This needs to look like a mugging gone bad, not a shoot-out."

Dempsey clenched his jaw in irritation and stood there motionless, sighting over his Sig at the entrance. For the first time in his long and decorated career, he was experiencing tactical paralysis . . .

Tactical paralysis in a petting zoo, he thought. *God, what have I become?*

He crept back to a position with a perpendicular firing angle on the enclosure. The side walls didn't have any windows, just a series of drilled ventilation holes that would be virtually impossible to sight and fire through.

I need a distraction, he decided.

He scanned the ground until he found a rock the size of his fist. He knelt and picked it up.

"Fuck it," he murmured, looking at the rock, and then lobbed it in a high arc at the shelter.

The rock hit the metal roof dead center with a loud, metallic clang that echoed through the park. Terrified sheep poured out of the enclosure in a wooly, stinky stampede—bleating, stomping, and defecating en masse. At the same time, Dempsey jumped the perimeter fence and charged forward in a low crouch. A sheep screamed to his left. The animal's cry was so uncannily human that he reflexively swiveled and sighted before dismissing the threat.

He pivoted back toward the enclosure doorway and felt the shift he'd been waiting for into the combat slipstream where all anxiety, uncertainty, and doubt evaporated. His mind and body unified into a state of hyperawareness and fluidity. With his weapon up in a two-handed grip and index finger tension on the trigger, he closed on the doorway. Then something happened he did not expect . . .

The sheep recoalesced into a compact herd and charged back toward the enclosure—apparently collectively deciding it was safer back inside than out here with him. On instinct, he went with them. Ducking as low as possible, he grabbed a fistful of wool on the back of a fat ewe and went in behind her like she was his blocking fullback. As he broke the plane of the doorway, he pulled the sheep tight to his chest, dug in his heels, and revectored her momentum radially. As they rotated in place, he scanned over her back for anything human-shaped in the shadows.

Collateral

A crack of gunfire exploded inside the metal structure, three deafening bangs along with three brilliant muzzle flashes from the back right corner. His sheep-shield bleated and shuddered—a fat wooly bullet cushion—as it took all three of the rounds. Dempsey returned fire, two rounds of his own into the corner, but the Russian was already rolling right and the slugs punched two holes harmlessly in the wall. Dempsey's ovine bodyguard suddenly became dead weight as the sheep's legs buckled. Its decision to die in that instant was unfortunate for Dempsey, because the Russian squeezed off another round. This one hit Dempsey center mass, square between his pecs. Instead of the familiar impact jab he was accustomed to when taking a round in Kevlar, he felt a sharp rippling tension across the breadth of his chest and then nothing.

The bullet had gone through his vest like a knife through butter.

Motherfucker, he thought as he returned fire at the Russian shadow. *I knew this shit was too good to be true.*

He scrambled right in the chaos—the gunfire having sent the sheep into blind pandemonium. Any second now, his breath would grow wet and raspy as his chest filled with blood. His blood pressure would drop, his arms would grow impossibly heavy, and his legs would turn to jelly. But none of those things happened. Was it possible that Baldwin's vest full of magic slime had actually friggin' worked?

Still strong and in the fight, Dempsey grabbed a fleeing ewe—smaller than the last—and ducked down behind her. Instead of firing over her back, he sighted around her ass. Muzzle flashes lit up the inside the shelter as the Russian emptied his magazine. Multiple rounds slammed into Dempsey's sheep, and it sprayed the side of his face with shit pellets. He returned fire, aiming just below the muzzle flashes.

Crack, crack, crack . . .

A human-shaped shadow dropped, hitting the dirt with a thud.

Dempsey released his grip on his second sheep, and the ewe collapsed beside him. He shifted from a crouch to a tactical knee, his Sig trained on his target, with whom he was finally alone in the barn. The Russian groaned and wheezed as he made a futile belly crawl toward the pistol he'd dropped, now a meter away.

"Stop," Dempsey said in Russian, surprised how the word came to him automatically. He'd been taking lessons from Buz—who claimed Dempsey had the worst language skills of anyone he'd ever taught. This was the first time the language had come to him without trying.

The Russian stopped and strained a backward look at him.

Collateral

Dempsey pressed to his feet and walked over to the man, keeping a proper standoff in case the Russian operator wasn't quite as wounded as he was letting on. The two men locked eyes, victor and vanquished.

The spy said something to him, but the only word he caught was "Zhukov." It didn't matter, though, because he knew his enemy well enough to infer the question. Dempsey was hunting Zetas—the Russian Federation's most secret and lethal black ops task force—taking them out one by one until he'd worked his way to the top.

"No, Zhukov didn't send me," Dempsey said, answering in English this time. "Shane Smith did."

Confusion washed over the other man's face, the murdered Ember Director's name clearly unknown to him. Dempsey wasn't surprised; only one Zeta had survived the horrific attack ordered by Russian spymaster Arkady Zhukov on Ember's secret compound in Virginia three months ago. Apparently, this dude wasn't that guy.

"De oppresso liber, comrade," he said and squeezed the trigger, completing the mission and ending the life of yet another Zeta.

"Well, that certainly didn't go as planned," Baldwin said in his ear as the last wisp of smoke from Dempsey's muzzle faded into the ether.

Where there had been only one siren wailing before, now a chorus screamed in the night.

"What do you want me to do with the body?" Dempsey asked.

"Leave it," Baldwin said through a defeated sigh. "And you can explain to the DNI why you violated the OPORD."

"Roger that," he said, holstering his weapon as he ducked out of the barn.

"Exfil north," Grimes said in his ear. "I'll pick you up in the Asda superstore parking lot."

"Check."

"Hurry, they're coming," she said.

"I *know*," he said, a surge of fresh adrenaline helping get his sluggish legs moving. And as he ran, thoughts of the next mission began to take shape. "Hey, Omega?"

"What is it, Alpha?" Baldwin answered, still irritated.

A malign smile curled Dempsey's lips.

"I'm ready for the next target."

TO BE NOTIFIED WHEN BRIAN AND JEFF'S BOOKS ARE AVAILABLE FOR PREORDER AND/OR SALE, SIGN UP FOR THEIR NEWSLETTER AT:

http://www.andrews-wilson.com

OR FOLLOW THEIR AUTHOR PAGES AT:

Amazon
https://www.amazon.com/Jeffrey-Wilson/e/B0034NOJ2K
https://www.amazon.com/Brian-Andrews/e/B0064GVLR0

BookBub
https://www.bookbub.com/authors/jeffrey-wilson
https://www.bookbub.com/authors/brian-andrews

Goodreads
https://www.goodreads.com/jeffreywilson
https://www.goodreads.com/brianandrews

Facebook
https://www.facebook.com/andrewsandwilson

Twitter
https://twitter.com/BAndrewsJWilson
https://twitter.com/JWilsonWarTorn
https://twitter.com/lexicalforge

ABOUT THE AUTHORS

BRIAN ANDREWS is a US Navy veteran, Park Leadership Fellow, and former submarine officer with degrees from Vanderbilt and Cornell Universities. He is the author of three critically acclaimed high-tech thrillers: *Reset*, *The Infiltration Game*, and *The Calypso Directive*.

JEFFREY WILSON has worked as an actor, firefighter, paramedic, jet pilot, and diving instructor, as well as a vascular and trauma surgeon. He served in the US Navy for fourteen years and made multiple deployments as a combat surgeon with an East Coast–based SEAL Team. The author of the faith-based inspirational war novel *War Torn* and three award-winning supernatural thrillers, *The Traiteur's Ring*, *The Donors*, and *Fade to Black*, he and his wife, Wendy, live in Southwest Florida with their four children.

Printed in Great Britain
by Amazon